THE ROOM IN THE DRAGON VOLANT

THE ROOM IN THE DRAGON VOLANT

J. S. Le Fanu

Skeptic Press

First published by Richard Bentley and Son 1872.

Skeptic Press
www.skepticpress.com

Publisher's Note: This is a work of fiction. Names, characters, places, and incidents are a product of the author's imagination. Locales and public names are sometimes used for atmospheric purposes. Any resemblance to actual people, living or dead, or to businesses, companies, events, institutions, or locales is completely coincidental.

Ordering Information:
Quantity sales. Special discounts are available on quantity purchases by corporations, associations, and others. For details, contact the publisher at the website listed above.

The Room in the Dragon Volant/ Joseph Sheridan Le Fanu.
ISBN 978-0-9790156-3-2

The intellect is always fooled by the heart.

—FRANCOIS DE LA ROCHEFAUCAULD

PROLOGUE

The curious case which I am about to place before you, is referred to, very pointedly, and more than once, in the extraordinary *Essay upon the Drug of the Dark and the Middle Ages*, from the pen of Doctor Hesselius.

This Essay he entitles *Mortis Imago*, and he, therein, discusses the Vinum letiferum, the Beatifica, the Somnus Angelorum, the Hypnus Sagarum, the Aqua Thessalliae, and about twenty other infusions and distillations, well known to the sages of eight hundred years ago, and two of which are still, he alleges, known to the fraternity of thieves, and, among them, as police-office inquiries sometimes disclose to this day, in practical use.

The Essay, *Mortis Imago*, will occupy, as nearly as I can at present calculate, two volumes, the ninth and tenth, of the collected papers of Dr. Martin Hesselius.

This Essay, I may remark in conclusion, is very curiously enriched by citations, in great abundance, from medieval verse and prose romance, some of the most valuable of which, strange to say, are Egyptian.

I have selected this particular statement from among many cases equally striking, but hardly, I think, so effective as mere narratives; in this irregular form of publication, it is simply as a story that I present it.

--*Joseph Sheridan Le Fanu*

CHAPTER ONE

ON THE ROAD

In the eventful year, 1815, I was exactly three-and-twenty, and had just succeeded to a very large sum in consols and other securities. The first fall of Napoleon had thrown the continent open to English excursionists, anxious, let us suppose, to improve their minds by foreign travel; and I—the slight check of the "hundred days" removed, by the genius of Wellington, on the field of Waterloo—was now added to the philosophic throng.

I was posting up to Paris from Brussels, following, I presume, the route that the allied army had pursued but a few weeks before—more carriages than you could believe were pursuing the same line. You could not look back or forward, without seeing into far perspective the clouds of dust, which marked the line of the long series of vehicles. We were perpetually passing relays of return-horses, on their way, jaded and dusty, to the inns from which they had been taken. They were arduous times for those patient public servants. The whole world seemed posting up to Paris.

I ought to have noted it more particularly, but my head was so full of Paris and the future that I passed the intervening scenery with little patience and less attention; I think, however, that it was about four miles to the frontier side of a rather picturesque little town, the name of which, as of many more important places through which I posted in my hurried journey, I forget, and about two hours before sunset, that we came up with a carriage in distress.

It was not quite an upset. But the two leaders were lying flat. The booted postilions had got down, and two servants who seemed very much at sea in such matters, were by way of assisting them. A pretty little bonnet and head were popped out of the window of the carriage in distress. Its *tournure,* and that of the shoulders that also appeared for a moment, was captivating: I resolved to play the part of a good Samaritan; stopped my chaise, jumped out, and with my servant lent a very willing hand in the emergency. Alas! the lady with the pretty bonnet wore a very thick black veil. I could see nothing but the pattern of the Brussels lace as she drew back.

A lean old gentleman, almost at the same time, stuck his head out of the window. An invalid he seemed, for although the day was hot he wore a black muffler which came up to his ears and nose, quite covering the lower part of his face, an arrangement which he disturbed by pulling it down for a moment, and poured forth a torrent of French thanks, as he uncovered his black wig, and gesticulated with grateful animation.

One of my very few accomplishments, besides boxing, which was cultivated by all Englishmen at that time, was French; and I replied, I hope and believe grammatically. Many bows being exchanged, the old gentleman's head went in again, and the demure, pretty little bonnet once more appeared.

The lady must have heard me speak to my servant, for she framed her little speech in such pretty, broken English, and in a voice so sweet, that I more than ever cursed the black veil that baulked my romantic curiosity.

The arms that were emblazoned on the panel were peculiar; I remember especially one device—it was the figure of a stork, painted in carmine, upon what the heralds call a "field or." The bird was standing upon one leg, and in the other claw held a stone. This is, I believe, the emblem of vigilance. Its oddity struck me, and remained impressed upon my memory. There were supporters besides, but I forget what they were. The courtly manners of these people, the style of their servants, the elegance of their traveling carriage, and the supporters to their arms, satisfied me that they were noble.

The lady, you may be sure, was not the less interesting on that account. What a fascination a title exercises upon the imagination! I do not mean on that of snobs or moral flunkies. Superiority of rank is a powerful and genuine influence in love. The idea of superior refinement is associated with it. The careless notice of the squire tells more upon the heart of the pretty milk maid than years of honest Dobbin's manly devotion, and so on and up. It is an unjust world!

But in this case there was something more. I was conscious of being good-looking. I really believe I was; and there could be no mistake about my being nearly six feet high. Why need this lady have thanked me? Had not her husband, for such I assumed him to be, thanked me quite enough and for both? I was instinctively aware that the lady was looking on me with no unwilling eyes; and, through her veil, I felt the power of her gaze.

She was now rolling away, with a train of dust behind her wheels in the golden sunlight, and a wise young gentleman followed her with ardent eyes and sighed profoundly as the distance increased.

I told the postilions on no account to pass the carriage, but to keep it steadily in view, and to pull up at whatever posting-house it should stop at. We were soon in the little town, and the carriage we followed drew up at the Belle Étoile, a comfortable old inn. They got out of the carriage and entered the house.

At a leisurely pace we followed. I got down, and mounted the steps listlessly, like a man quite apathetic and careless.

Audacious as I was, I did not care to inquire in what room I should find them. I peeped into the apartment to my right, and then into that on my left. *My* people were not there. I ascended the stairs. A drawing-room door stood open. I entered with the most innocent air in the world. It was a spacious room, and, beside myself, contained but one living figure—a very pretty and lady-like one. There was the very bonnet with which I had fallen in love. The lady stood with her back toward me. I could not tell whether the envious veil was raised; she was reading a letter.

I stood for a minute in fixed attention, gazing upon her, in vague hope that she might turn about and give me an opportunity of seeing her features. She did not; but with a step or two she placed herself before a little cabriole-table, which stood against the wall, from which rose a tall mirror in a tarnished frame.

I might, indeed, have mistaken it for a picture; for it now reflected a half-length portrait of a singularly beautiful woman.

She was looking down upon a letter which she held in her slender fingers, and in which she seemed absorbed.

The face was oval, melancholy, sweet. It had in it, nevertheless, a faint and undefinably sensual quality also. Nothing could exceed the delicacy of its features, or the brilliancy of its tints. The eyes, indeed, were lowered, so that I could not see their color; nothing but their long lashes and delicate eyebrows. She continued reading. She must have been deeply interested; I never saw a living form so motionless—I gazed on a tinted statue.

Being at that time blessed with long and keen vision, I saw this beautiful face with perfect distinctness. I saw even the blue veins that traced their wanderings on the whiteness of her full throat.

I ought to have retreated as noiselessly as I came in, before my presence was detected. But I was too much interested to move from the spot, for a few moments longer; and while they were passing, she raised her eyes. Those eyes were large, and of that hue which modern poets term "violet."

These splendid melancholy eyes were turned upon me from the glass, with a haughty stare, and hastily the lady lowered her black veil, and turned about.

I fancied that she hoped I had not seen her. I was watching every look and movement, the minutest, with an attention as intense as if an ordeal involving my life depended on them.

CHAPTER TWO

THE INN-YARD OF THE BELLE ÉTOILE

The face was, indeed, one to fall in love with at first sight. Those sentiments that take such sudden possession of young men were now dominating my curiosity. My audacity faltered before her; and I felt that my presence in this room was probably an impertinence. This point she quickly settled, for the same very sweet voice I had heard before, now said coldly, and this time in French, "Monsieur cannot be aware that this apartment is not public."

I bowed very low, faltered some apologies, and backed to the door.

I suppose I looked penitent, and embarrassed. I certainly felt so; for the lady said, by way it seemed of softening matters, "I am happy, however, to have an opportunity of again thanking Monsieur for the assistance, so prompt and effectual, which he had the goodness to render us today."

It was more the altered tone in which it was spoken, than the speech itself, that encouraged me. It was also true that she need not have recognized me; and if she had, she certainly was not obliged to thank me over again.

All this was indescribably flattering, and all the more so that it followed so quickly on her slight reproof. The tone in which she spoke had become low and timid, and I observed that she turned her head quickly towards a second door of the room; I fancied that the gentleman in the black wig, a jealous husband perhaps, might reappear through it. Almost at the same moment, a voice at once reedy and nasal was heard snarling some directions to a servant, and evidently approaching. It was the voice that had thanked me so profusely, from the carriage windows, about an hour before.

"Monsieur will have the goodness to retire," said the lady, in a tone that resembled entreaty, at the same time gently waving her hand toward the door through which I had entered. Bowing again very low, I stepped back, and closed the door.

I ran down the stairs, very much elated. I saw the host of the Belle Étoile which, as I said, was the sign and designation of my inn.

I described the apartment I had just quitted, said I liked it, and asked whether I could have it.

He was extremely troubled, but that apartment and two adjoining rooms were engaged.

"By whom?"

"People of distinction."

"But who are they? They must have names or titles."

"Undoubtedly, Monsieur, but such a stream is rolling into Paris, that we have ceased to inquire the names or titles of our guests—we designate them simply by the rooms they occupy."

"What stay do they make?"

"Even that, Monsieur, I cannot answer. It does not interest us. Our rooms, while this continues, can never be, for a moment, disengaged."

"I should have liked those rooms so much! Is one of them a sleeping apartment?"

"Yes, sir, and Monsieur will observe that people do not usually engage bedrooms unless they mean to stay the night."

"Well, I can, I suppose, have some rooms, any, I don't care in what part of the house?"

"Certainly, Monsieur can have two apartments. They are the last at present disengaged."

I took them instantly.

It was plain these people meant to make a stay here; at least they would not go till morning. I began to feel that I was all but engaged in an adventure.

I took possession of my rooms, and looked out of the window, which I found commanded the inn-yard. Many horses were being liberated from the traces, hot and weary, and others fresh from the stables being put to. A great many vehicles—some private carriages, others, like mine, of that public class which is equivalent to our old English post-chaise, were standing on the pavement, waiting their turn for relays. Fussy servants were to-ing and fro-ing, and idle ones lounging or laughing, and the scene, on the whole, was animated and amusing.

Among these objects, I thought I recognized the traveling carriage, and one of the servants of the "persons of distinction" about whom I was, just then, so profoundly interested.

I therefore ran down the stairs, made my way to the back door; and so, behold me, in a moment, upon the uneven pavement, among all these sights and sounds which in such a place attend upon a period of extraordinary crush and traffic. By this time the sun was near its setting, and threw its golden beams on the red brick chimneys of the offices, and made the two barrels, that figured as pigeon-houses, on the tops of poles, look as if they were on fire. Everything in this light becomes picturesque; and things interest us which, in the sober grey of morning, are dull enough.

After a little search I lighted upon the very carriage of which I was in quest. A servant was locking one of the doors, for it was made with the security of lock and key. I paused near, looking at the panel of the door.

"A very pretty device that red stork!" I observed, pointing to the shield on the door, "and no doubt indicates a distinguished family?"

The servant looked at me for a moment, as he placed the little key in his pocket, and said with a slightly sarcastic bow and smile, "Monsieur is at liberty to conjecture."

Nothing daunted, I forthwith administered that laxative which, on occasion, acts so happily upon the tongue—I mean a "tip."

The servant looked at the Napoleon in his hand, and then in my face, with a sincere expression of surprise. "Monsieur is very generous!"

"Not worth mentioning—who are the lady and gentleman who came here in this carriage, and whom, you may remember, I and my servant assisted today in an emergency, when their horses had come to the ground?"

"They are the Count, and the young lady we call the Countess—but I know not, she may be his daughter."

"Can you tell me where they live?"

"Upon my honor, Monsieur, I am unable—I know not."

"Not know where your master lives! Surely you know something more about him than his name?"

"Nothing worth relating, Monsieur; in fact, I was hired in Brussels, on the very day they started. Monsieur Picard, my fellow servant, Monsieur the Comte's gentleman, he has been years in his service, and knows everything; but he never speaks except to communicate an order. From him I have learned nothing. We are going to Paris, however, and there I shall speedily pick up all about them. At present I am as ignorant of all that as Monsieur himself."

"And where is Monsieur Picard?"

"He has gone to the cutler's to get his razors set. But I do not think he will tell anything."

This was a poor harvest for my golden sowing. The man, I think, spoke truth, and would honestly have betrayed the secrets of the family, if he had possessed any. I took my leave politely; and mounting the stairs again, I found myself once more in my room.

Forthwith I summoned my servant. Though I had brought him with me from England, he was a native of France—a useful fellow, sharp, bustling, and, of course, quite familiar with the ways and tricks of his countrymen.

"St. Clair, shut the door; come here. I can't rest till I have made out something about those people of rank who have got the apartments under mine. Here are fifteen francs; make out the servants we assisted today have them to a petit souper, and come back and tell me their entire history. I have, this moment, seen one of them who knows nothing, and has communicated it. The other, whose name I forget, is the unknown nobleman's valet, and knows everything. Him you must pump. It is, of course, the venerable peer, and not the young lady who accompanies him, that interests me—you understand? Begone! fly! and return with all the details I sigh for, and every circumstance that can possibly interest me."

It was a commission which admirably suited the tastes and spirits of my worthy St. Clair, to whom, you will have observed, I had accustomed myself to talk with the peculiar familiarity which the old French comedy establishes between master and valet.

I am sure he laughed at me in secret; but nothing could be more polite and deferential.

With several wise looks, nods and shrugs, he withdrew; and looking down from my window, I saw him with incredible quickness enter the yard, where I soon lost sight of him among the carriages.

CHAPTER THREE

DEATH AND LOVE TOGETHER MATED

When the day drags, when a man is solitary, and in a fever of impatience and suspense; when the minute hand of his watch travels as slowly as the hour hand used to do, and the hour hand has lost all appreciable motion; when he yawns, and beats the devil's tattoo, and flattens his handsome nose against the window, and whistles tunes he hates, and, in short, does not know what to do with himself, it is deeply to be regretted that he cannot make a solemn dinner of three courses more than once in a day. The laws of matter, to which we are slaves, deny us that resource.

But in the times I speak of, supper was still a substantial meal, and its hour was approaching. This was consolatory. Three-quarters of an hour, however, still interposed. How was I to dispose of that interval?

I had two or three idle books, it is true, as companions; but there are many moods in which one cannot read. My novel lay with my rug and walking-stick on the sofa, and I did not care if the heroine and the hero were both drowned together in the water barrel that I saw in the inn-yard under my window. I took a turn or two up and down my room, and sighed, looking at myself in the glass, adjusted my great white "choker," folded and tied after Brummel, the immortal "Beau," put on a buff waist-coat and my blue swallow-tailed coat with gilt buttons; I deluged my pocket-handkerchief with Eau-de-Cologne (we had not then the variety of bouquets with which the genius of perfumery has since blessed us) I arranged my hair, on which I piqued myself, and which I loved to groom in those days. That dark-brown *chevelure,* with a natural curl, is now represented by a few dozen perfectly white hairs, and its place—a smooth, bald, pink head—knows it no more. But let us forget these mortifications. It was then rich, thick, and dark-brown. I was making a very careful toilet. I took my unexceptionable hat from its case, and placed it lightly on my wise head, as nearly as memory and practice enabled me to do so, at that very slight inclination which the immortal person I have mentioned was wont to give to his. A pair of light French gloves and a rather club-like knotted walking-stick, such as just then came into vogue for a year or two again in England, in the phraseology of Sir Walter Scott's romances "completed my equipment."

All this attention to effect, preparatory to a mere lounge in the yard, or on the steps of the Belle Étoile, was a simple act of devotion to the wonderful eyes which I had that evening beheld for the first time, and never, never could forget! In plain terms, it was all done in the vague, very vague hope that those eyes might behold the unexceptionable get-up of a melancholy slave, and retain the image, not altogether without secret approbation.

As I completed my preparations the light failed me; the last level streak of sunlight disappeared, and a fading twilight only remained. I sighed in unison with the pensive hour, and threw open the window, intending to look out for a moment before going downstairs. I perceived instantly that the window underneath mine was also open, for I heard two voices in conversation, although I could not distinguish what they were saying.

The male voice was peculiar; it was, as I told you, reedy and nasal. I knew it, of course, instantly. The answering voice spoke in those sweet tones which I recognized only too easily. The dialogue was only for a minute; the repulsive male voice laughed, I fancied, with a kind of devilish satire, and retired from the window, so that I almost ceased to hear it.

The other voice remained nearer the window, but not so near as at first.

It was not an altercation; there was evidently nothing the least exciting in the colloquy. What would I not have given that it had been a quarrel—a violent one—and I the redresser of wrongs, and the defender of insulted beauty! Alas! so far as I could pronounce upon the character of the tones I heard, they might be as tranquil a pair as any in existence. In a moment more the lady began to sing an odd little chanson. I need not remind you how much farther the voice is heard singing than speaking. I could distinguish the words. The voice was of that exquisitely sweet kind which is called, I believe, a semi-contralto; it had something pathetic, and something, I fancied, a little mocking in its tones. I venture a clumsy, but adequate translation of the words:

"Death and Love, together mated,
  Watch and wait in ambuscade;
At early morn, or else belated,
  They meet and mark the man or maid.

Burning sigh, or breath that freezes,
  Numbs or maddens man or maid;
Death or Love the victim seizes,
  Breathing from their ambuscade."

"Enough, Madame!" said the old voice, with sudden severity. "We do not desire, I believe, to amuse the grooms and hostlers in the yard with our music."

The lady's voice laughed gaily.

"You desire to quarrel, Madame!" And the old man, I presume, shut down the window. Down it went, at all events, with a rattle that might easily have broken the glass.

Of all thin partitions, glass is the most effectual excluder of sound. I heard no more, not even the subdued hum of the colloquy.

What a charming voice this Countess had! How it melted, swelled, and trembled! How it moved, and even agitated me! What a pity that a hoarse old jackdaw should have power to crow down such a Philomel! "Alas! what a life it is!" I moralized, wisely. "That beautiful Countess, with the patience of an angel and the beauty of a Venus and the accomplishments of all the Muses, a slave! She knows perfectly who occupies the apartments over hers; she heard me raise my window. One may conjecture pretty well for whom that music was intended—aye, old gentleman, and for whom you suspected it to be intended."

In a very agreeable flutter I left my room and, descending the stairs, passed the Count's door very much at my leisure. There was just a chance that the beautiful songstress might emerge. I dropped my stick on the lobby, near their door, and you may be sure it took me some little time to pick it up! Fortune, nevertheless, did not favor me. I could not stay on the lobby all night picking up my stick, so I went down to the hall.

I consulted the clock, and found that there remained but a quarter of an hour to the moment of supper.

Everyone was roughing it now, every inn in confusion; people might do at such a juncture what they never did before. Was it just possible that, for once, the Count and Countess would take their chairs at the table-d'hôte?

CHAPTER FOUR

MONSIEUR DROQVILLE

Full of this exciting hope I sauntered out upon the steps of the Belle Étoile. It was now night, and a pleasant moonlight over everything. I had entered more into my romance since my arrival, and this poetic light heightened the sentiment. What a drama if she turned out to be the Count's daughter, and in love with me! What a delightful—*tragedy* if she turned out to be the Count's wife! In this luxurious mood I was accosted by a tall and very elegantly made gentleman, who appeared to be about fifty. His air was courtly and graceful, and there was in his whole manner and appearance something so distinguished that it was impossible not to suspect him of being a person of rank.

He had been standing upon the steps, looking out, like me, upon the moonlight effects that transformed, as it were, the objects and buildings in the little street. He accosted me, I say, with the politeness, at once easy and lofty, of a French nobleman of the old school. He asked me if I were not Mr. Beckett? I assented; and he immediately introduced himself as the Marquis d'Harmonville (this information he gave me in a low tone), and asked leave to present me with a letter from Lord R——, who knew my father slightly, and had once done me, also, a trifling kindness.

This English peer, I may mention, stood very high in the political world, and was named as the most probable successor to the distinguished post of English Minister at Paris. I received it with a low bow, and read:

> My Dear Beckett,
>
> I beg to introduce my very dear friend, the Marquis d'Harmonville, who will explain to you the nature of the services it may be in your power to render him and us.

He went on to speak of the Marquis as a man whose great wealth, whose intimate relations with the old families, and whose legitimate influence with the court rendered him the fittest possible person for those friendly offices which, at the desire of his own sovereign, and of our government, he has so obligingly undertaken. It added a great deal to my perplexity, when I read, further:

> By-the-bye, Walton was here yesterday, and told me that your seat was likely to be attacked; something, he says, is unquestionably going on at Domwell. You know there is an awkwardness in my meddling ever so cautiously. But I advise, if it is not very officious, your making Haxton look after it and report immediately. I fear it is serious. I ought to have mentioned that, for reasons that you will see, when you have talked with him for five minutes, the Marquis—with the concurrence of all our friends—drops his title, for a few weeks, and is at present plain Monsieur Droqville. I am this moment going to town, and can say no more.
>
> Yours faithfully,
>
> R——

I was utterly puzzled. I could scarcely boast of Lord R——'s acquaintance. I knew no one named Haxton, and, except my hatter, no one called Walton; and this peer wrote as if we were intimate friends! I looked at the back of the letter, and the mystery was solved. And now, to my consternation—for I was plain Richard Beckett—I read:

"To George Stanhope Beckett, Esq., M.P."

I looked with consternation in the face of the Marquis.

"What apology can I offer to Monsieur the Mar—— to Monsieur Droqville? It is true my name is Beckett—it is true I am known, though very slightly, to Lord R——; but the letter was not intended for me. My name is Richard Beckett—this is to Mr. Stanhope Beckett, the member for Shillingsworth. What can I say, or do, in this unfortunate situation? I can only give you my honor as a gentleman, that, for me, the letter, which I now return, shall remain as unviolated a secret as before I opened it. I am so shocked and grieved that such a mistake should have occurred!"

I dare say my honest vexation and good faith were pretty legibly written in my countenance; for the look of gloomy embarrassment which had for a moment settled on the face of the Marquis, brightened; he smiled, kindly, and extended his hand.

"I have not the least doubt that Monsieur Beckett will respect my little secret. As a mistake was destined to occur, I have reason to thank my good stars that it should have been with a gentleman of honor. Monsieur Beckett will permit me, I hope, to place his name among those of my friends?"

I thanked the Marquis very much for his kind expressions. He went on to say:

"If, Monsieur, I can persuade you to visit me at Claironville, in Normandy, where I hope to see, on the 15th of August, a great many friends, whose acquaintance it might interest you to make, I shall be too happy."

I thanked him, of course, very gratefully for his hospitality. He continued: "I cannot, for the present, see my friends, for reasons which you may surmise, at my house in Paris. But Monsieur will be so good as to let me know the hotel he means to stay at in Paris; and he will find that although the Marquis d'Harmonville is not in town, that Monsieur Droqville will not lose sight of him."

With many acknowledgments I gave him the information he desired.

"And in the meantime," he continued, "if you think of any way in which Monsieur Droqville can be of use to you, our communication shall not be interrupted, and I shall so manage matters that you can easily let me know."

I was very much flattered. The Marquis had, as we say, taken a fancy to me. Such likings at first sight often ripen into lasting friendships. To be sure it was just possible that the Marquis might think it prudent to keep the involuntary depositary of a political secret, even so vague a one, in good humor.

Very graciously the Marquis took his leave, going up the stairs of the Belle Étoile.

I remained upon the steps for a minute, lost in speculation upon this new theme of interest. But the wonderful eyes, the thrilling voice, the exquisite figure of the beautiful lady who had taken possession of my imagination, quickly reasserted their influence. I was again gazing at the sympathetic moon, and descending the steps I loitered along the pavements among strange objects, and houses that were antique and picturesque, in a dreamy state, thinking.

In a little while I turned into the inn-yard again. There had come a lull. Instead of the noisy place it was an hour or two before, the yard was perfectly still and empty, except for the carriages that stood here and there. Perhaps there was a servants' table-d'hôte just then. I was rather pleased to find solitude; and undisturbed I found out my lady-love's carriage, in the moonlight. I mused, I walked round it; I was as utterly foolish and maudlin as very young men, in my situation, usually are. The blinds were down, the doors, I suppose, locked. The brilliant moonlight revealed everything, and cast sharp, black shadows of wheel, and bar, and spring, on the pavement. I stood before the escutcheon painted on the door, which I had examined in the daylight. I wondered how often her eyes had rested on the same object. I pondered in a charming dream. A harsh, loud voice, over my shoulder, said suddenly: "A red stork—

good! The stork is a bird of prey; it is vigilant, greedy, and catches gudgeons. Red, too!—blood red! Ha ha! the symbol is appropriate."

I had turned about, and beheld the palest face I ever saw. It was broad, ugly, and malignant. The figure was that of a French officer, in undress, and was six feet high. Across the nose and eyebrow there was a deep scar, which made the repulsive face grimmer.

The officer elevated his chin and his eyebrows, with a scoffing chuckle, and said: "I have shot a stork, with a rifle bullet, when he thought himself safe in the clouds, for mere sport!" (He shrugged, and laughed malignantly.) "See, Monsieur; when a man like me—a man of energy, you understand, a man with all his wits about him, a man who has made the tour of Europe under canvas, and, parbleu! often without it— resolves to discover a secret, expose a crime, catch a thief, spit a robber on the point of his sword, it is odd if he does not succeed. Ha! ha! ha! Adieu, Monsieur!"

He turned with an angry whisk on his heel, and swaggered with long strides out of the gate.

CHAPTER FIVE

SUPPER AT THE BELLE ÉTOILE

The French army were in a rather savage temper just then. The English, especially, had but scant courtesy to expect at their hands. It was plain, however, that the cadaverous gentleman who had just apostrophized the heraldry of the Count's carriage, with such mysterious acrimony, had not intended any of his malevolence for me. He was stung by some old recollection, and had marched off, seething with fury.

I had received one of those unacknowledged shocks which startle us, when, fancying ourselves perfectly alone, we discover on a sudden that our antics have been watched by a spectator, almost at our elbow. In this case the effect was enhanced by the extreme repulsiveness of the face, and, I may add, its proximity, for, as I think, it almost touched mine. The enigmatical harangue of this person, so full of hatred and implied denunciation, was still in my ears. Here at all events was new matter for the industrious fancy of a lover to work upon.

It was time now to go to the table-d'hôte. Who could tell what lights the gossip of the supper-table might throw upon the subject that interested me so powerfully!

I stepped into the room, my eyes searching the little assembly, about thirty people, for the persons who specially interested me. It was not easy to induce people, so hurried and overworked as those of the Belle

Étoile just now, to send meals up to one's private apartments, in the midst of this unparalleled confusion; and, therefore, many people who did not like it might find themselves reduced to the alternative of supping at the table-d'hôte or starving.

The Count was not there, nor his beautiful companion; but the Marquis d'Harmonville, whom I hardly expected to see in so public a place, signed, with a significant smile, to a vacant chair beside himself. I secured it, and he seemed pleased, and almost immediately entered into conversation with me.

"This is, probably, your first visit to France?" he said.

I told him it was, and he said:

"You must not think me very curious and impertinent; but Paris is about the most dangerous capital a high-spirited and generous young gentleman could visit without a Mentor. If you have not an experienced friend as a companion during your visit—." He paused.

I told him I was not so provided, but that I had my wits about me; that I had seen a good deal of life in England, and that I fancied human nature was pretty much the same in all parts of the world. The Marquis shook his head, smiling.

"You will find very marked differences, notwithstanding," he said. "Peculiarities of intellect and peculiarities of character, undoubtedly, do pervade different nations; and this results, among the criminal classes, in a style of villainy no less peculiar. In Paris the class who live by their wits is three or four times as great as in London; and they live much better; some of them even splendidly. They are more ingenious than the London rogues; they have more animation and invention, and the dramatic faculty, in which your countrymen are deficient, is everywhere. These invaluable attributes place them upon a totally different level. They can affect the manners and enjoy the luxuries of people of distinction. They live, many of them, by play."

"So do many of our London rogues."

"Yes, but in a totally different way. They are the *habitués* of certain gaming-tables, billiard-rooms, and other places, including your races, where high play goes on; and by superior knowledge of chances, by masking their play, by means of confederates, by means of bribery, and other artifices, varying with the subject of their imposture, they rob the unwary. But here it is more elaborately done, and with a really exquisite *finesse.* There are people whose manners, style, conversation, are unexceptionable, living in handsome houses in the best situations, with everything about them in the most refined taste, and exquisitely luxurious, who impose even upon the Parisian bourgeois, who believe them to be, in good faith, people of rank and fashion, because their habits are expensive and refined, and their houses are frequented by foreigners of distinction, and, to a degree, by foolish young Frenchmen of rank. At all these houses play goes on. The ostensible host and hostess seldom join in it; they provide it simply to plunder their guests, by means of their accomplices, and thus wealthy strangers are inveigled and robbed."

"But I have heard of a young Englishman, a son of Lord Rooksbury, who broke two Parisian gaming tables only last year."

"I see," he said, laughing, "you are come here to do likewise. I, myself, at about your age, undertook the same spirited enterprise. I raised no less a sum than five hundred thousand francs to begin with; I expected to carry all before me by the simple expedient of going on doubling my stakes. I had heard of it, and I fancied that the sharpers, who kept the table, knew nothing of the matter. I found, however, that they not only knew all about it, but had provided against the possibility of any such experiments; and I was pulled up before I had well begun by a rule which forbids the doubling of an original stake more than four times consecutively."

"And is that rule in force still?" I inquired, chapfallen.

He laughed and shrugged, "Of course it is, my young friend. People who live by an art always understand it better than an amateur. I see you had formed the same plan, and no doubt came provided."

I confessed I had prepared for conquest upon a still grander scale. I had arrived with a purse of thirty thousand pounds sterling.

"Any acquaintance of my very dear friend, Lord R——, interests me; and, besides my regard for him, I am charmed with you; so you will pardon all my, perhaps, too officious questions and advice."

I thanked him most earnestly for his valuable counsel, and begged that he would have the goodness to give me all the advice in his power.

"Then if you take my advice," said he, "you will leave your money in the bank where it lies. Never risk a Napoleon in a gaming house. The night I went to break the bank I lost between seven and eight thousand pounds sterling of your English money; and my next adventure, I had obtained an introduction to one of those elegant gaming-houses which affect to be the private mansions of persons of distinction, and was saved from ruin by a gentleman whom, ever since, I have regarded with increasing respect and friendship. It oddly happens he is in this house at this moment. I recognized his servant, and made him a visit in his apartments here, and found him the same brave, kind, honorable man I always knew him. But that he is living so entirely out of the world, now, I should have made a point of introducing you. Fifteen years ago he would have been the man of all others to consult. The gentleman I speak of is the Comte de St. Alyre. He represents a very old family. He is the very soul of honor, and the most sensible man in the world, except in one particular."

"And that particular?" I hesitated. I was now deeply interested.

"Is that he has married a charming creature, at least five-and-forty years younger than himself, and is, of course, although I believe absolutely without cause, horribly jealous."

"And the lady?"

"The Countess is, I believe, in every way worthy of so good a man," he answered, a little dryly. "I think I heard her sing this evening."

"Yes, I daresay; she is very accomplished." After a few moments' silence he continued.

"I must not lose sight of you, for I should be sorry, when next you meet my friend Lord R——, that you had to tell him you had been pigeoned in Paris. A rich Englishman as you are, with so large a sum at his Paris bankers, young, gay, generous, a thousand ghouls and harpies will be contending who shall be the first to seize and devour you."

At this moment I received something like a jerk from the elbow of the gentleman at my right. It was an accidental jog, as he turned in his seat.

"On the honor of a soldier, there is no man's flesh in this company heals so fast as mine."

The tone in which this was spoken was harsh and stentorian, and almost made me bounce. I looked round and recognized the officer whose large white face had half scared me in the inn-yard, wiping his mouth furiously, and then with a gulp of Magon, he went on:

"No one! It's not blood; it is ichor! it's miracle! Set aside stature, thew, bone, and muscle—set aside courage, and by all the angels of death, I'd fight a lion naked, and dash his teeth down his jaws with my fist, and flog him to death with his own tail! Set aside, I say, all those attributes, which I am allowed to possess, and I am worth six men in any campaign, for that one quality of healing as I do—rip me up, punch me through, tear me to tatters with bomb-shells, and nature has me whole again, while your tailor would fine-draw an old coat. *Parbleu*! gentlemen, if you saw me naked, you would laugh! Look at my hand, a saber-cut across the palm, to the bone, to save my head, taken up with three stitches, and five days afterwards I was playing ball with an English general, a prisoner in Madrid, against the wall of the convent of the Santa Maria de la Castita! At Arcola, by the great devil himself! that was an action. Every man there, gentlemen, swallowed as much smoke in five minutes as would smother you all in this room! I received, at the same moment, two musket balls in the thighs, a grape shot through the calf of my leg, a lance through my left shoulder, a piece of a shrapnel in the left deltoid, a bayonet through the cartilage of my right ribs, a cut that carried away a pound of flesh from my chest, and the better part of a congreve rocket on my forehead. Pretty well, ha, ha! and all while you'd say bah! and in eight days and a half I was making a forced march, without shoes, and only one gaiter, the life and soul of my company, and as sound as a roach!"

"Bravo! Bravissimo! Per Bacco! un gallant' uomo!" exclaimed, in a martial ecstasy, a fat little Italian, who manufactured toothpicks and wicker cradles on the island of Notre Dame; "your exploits shall resound through Europe! and the history of those wars should be written in your blood!"

"Never mind! a trifle!" exclaimed the soldier. "At Ligny, the other day, where we smashed the Prussians into ten hundred thousand milliards of atoms, a bit of a shell cut me across the leg and opened an artery. It was spouting as high as the chimney, and in half a minute I had lost enough to fill a pitcher. I must have expired in another minute, if I had not whipped off my sash like a flash of lightning, tied it round my leg above the wound, whipt a bayonet out of the back of a dead Prussian, and passing it under, made a tourniquet of it with a couple of twists, and so stayed the hemorrhage and saved my life. But, *sacrebleu*! gentlemen, I lost so much blood, I have been as pale as the bottom of a plate ever since. No matter. A trifle. Blood well spent, gentlemen." He applied himself now to his bottle of *vin ordinaire*.

The Marquis had closed his eyes, and looked resigned and disgusted, while all this was going on.

"Garçon," said the officer, for the first time speaking in a low tone over the back of his chair to the waiter; "who came in that traveling carriage, dark yellow and black, that stands in the middle of the yard, with

arms and supporters emblazoned on the door, and a red stork, as red as my facings?"

The waiter could not say.

The eye of the eccentric officer, who had suddenly grown grim and serious, and seemed to have abandoned the general conversation to other people, lighted, as it were accidentally, on me.

"Pardon me, Monsieur," he said. "Did I not see you examining the panel of that carriage at the same time that I did so, this evening? Can you tell me who arrived in it?"

"I rather think the Count and Countess de St. Alyre."

"And are they here, in the Belle Étoile?" he asked.

"They have got apartments upstairs," I answered.

He started up, and half pushed his chair from the table. He quickly sat down again, and I could hear him sacré-ing and muttering to himself, and grinning and scowling. I could not tell whether he was alarmed or furious.

I turned to say a word or two to the Marquis, but he was gone. Several other people had dropped out also, and the supper party soon broke up. Two or three substantial pieces of wood smoldered on the hearth, for the night had turned out chilly. I sat down by the fire in a great armchair of carved oak, with a marvelously high back that looked as old as the days of Henry IV.

"*Garçon,*" said I, "do you happen to know who that officer is?"

"That is Colonel Gaillarde, Monsieur."

"Has he been often here?"

"Once before, Monsieur, for a week; it is a year since."

"He is the palest man I ever saw."

"That is true, Monsieur; he has been often taken for a revenant."

"Can you give me a bottle of really good Burgundy?"

"The best in France, Monsieur."

"Place it, and a glass by my side, on this table, if you please. I may sit here for half-an-hour."

"Certainly, Monsieur."

I was very comfortable, the wine excellent, and my thoughts glowing and serene. "Beautiful Countess! Beautiful Countess! shall we ever be better acquainted?"

CHAPTER SIX

THE NAKED SWORD

A man who has been posting all day long, and changing the air he breathes every half hour, who is well pleased with himself, and has nothing on earth to trouble him, and who sits alone by a fire in a comfortable chair after having eaten a hearty supper, may be pardoned if he takes an accidental nap.

I had filled my fourth glass when I fell asleep. My head, I daresay, hung uncomfortably; and it is admitted that a variety of French dishes is not the most favorable precursor to pleasant dreams.

I had a dream as I took mine ease in mine inn on this occasion. I fancied myself in a huge cathedral, without light, except from four tapers that stood at the corners of a raised platform hung with black, on which lay, draped also in black, what seemed to me the dead body of the Countess de St. Alyre. The place seemed empty, it was cold, and I could see only (in the halo of the candles) a little way round.

The little I saw bore the character of Gothic gloom, and helped my fancy to shape and furnish the black void that yawned all round me. I heard a sound like the slow tread of two persons walking up the flagged aisle. A faint echo told of the vastness of the place. An awful sense of expectation was upon me, and I was horribly frightened when the body that lay on the catafalque said (without stirring), in a whisper that froze me, "They come to place me in the grave alive; save me."

I found that I could neither speak nor move. I was horribly frightened.

The two people who approached now emerged from the darkness. One, the Count de St. Alyre, glided to the head of the figure and placed his long thin hands under it. The white-faced Colonel, with the scar across his face, and a look of infernal triumph, placed his hands under her feet, and they began to raise her.

With an indescribable effort I broke the spell that bound me, and started to my feet with a gasp.

I was wide awake, but the broad, wicked face of Colonel Gaillarde was staring, white as death, at me from the other side of the hearth. "Where is she?" I shuddered.

"That depends on who she is, Monsieur," replied the Colonel, curtly.

"Good heavens!" I gasped, looking about me.

The Colonel, who was eyeing me sarcastically, had had his *demitasse* of *café noir*, and now drank his *tasse*, diffusing a pleasant perfume of brandy.

"I fell asleep and was dreaming," I said, lest any strong language, founded on the *rôle* he played in my dream, should have escaped me. "I did not know for some moments where I was."

"You are the young gentleman who has the apartments over the Count and Countess de St. Alyre?" he said, winking one eye, close in meditation, and glaring at me with the other.

"I believe so—yes," I answered.

"Well, younker, take care you have not worse dreams than that some night," he said, enigmatically, and wagged his head with a chuckle. "Worse dreams," he repeated.

"What does Monsieur the Colonel mean?" I inquired.

"I am trying to find that out myself," said the Colonel; "and I think I shall. When *I* get the first inch of the thread fast between my finger and thumb, it goes hard but I follow it up, bit by bit, little by little, tracing it this way and that, and up and down, and round about, until the whole clue is wound up on my thumb, and the end, and its secret, fast in my fingers. Ingenious! Crafty as five foxes! wide awake as a weasel! *Parbleu*! if I had descended to that occupation I should have made my fortune as a spy. Good wine here?" he glanced interrogatively at my bottle.

"Very good," said I. "Will Monsieur the Colonel try a glass?"

He took the largest he could find, and filled it, raised it with a bow, and drank it slowly. "Ah! ah! Bah! That is not it," he exclaimed, with some disgust, filling it again. "You ought to have told *me* to order your Burgundy, and they would not have brought you that stuff."

I got away from this man as soon as I civilly could, and, putting on my hat, I walked out with no other company than my sturdy walking-stick. I visited the inn-yard, and looked up to the windows of the Countess's apartments. They were closed, however, and I had not even the unsubstantial consolation of contemplating the light in which that beautiful lady was at that moment writing, or reading, or sitting and thinking of—anyone you please.

I bore this serious privation as well as I could, and took a little saunter through the town. I shan't bore you with moonlight effects, nor with the maunderings of a man who has fallen in love at first sight with a beautiful face. My ramble, it is enough to say, occupied about half an hour, and, returning by a slight détour, I found myself in a little square, with about two high gabled houses on each side, and a rude stone statue, worn by centuries of rain, on a pedestal in the center of the pavement. Looking at this statue was a slight and rather tall man, whom I instantly recognized as the Marquis d'Harmonville: he knew me almost as quickly. He walked a step towards me, shrugged and laughed:

"You are surprised to find Monsieur Droqville staring at that old stone figure by moonlight. Anything to pass the time. You, I see, suffer from *ennui*, as I do. These little provincial towns! Heavens! what an effort it is to live in them! If I could regret having formed in early life a friendship that does me honor, I think its condemning me to a sojourn in such a place would make me do so. You go on towards Paris, I suppose, in the morning?"

"I have ordered horses."

"As for me I await a letter, or an arrival, either would emancipate me; but I can't say how soon either event will happen."

"Can I be of any use in this matter?" I began.

"None, Monsieur, I thank you a thousand times. No, this is a piece in which every *rôle* is already cast. I am but an amateur, and induced solely by friendship, to take a part."

So he talked on, for a time, as we walked slowly toward the Belle Étoile, and then came a silence, which I broke by asking him if he knew anything of Colonel Gaillarde.

"Oh! yes, to be sure. He is a little mad; he has had some bad injuries of the head. He used to plague the people in the War Office to death. He has always some delusion. They contrived some employment for him—not regimental, of course—but in this campaign Napoleon, who could spare nobody, placed him in command of a regiment. He was always a desperate fighter, and such men were more than ever needed."

There is, or was, a second inn in this town called l'Écu de France. At its door the Marquis stopped, bade me a mysterious good-night, and disappeared.

As I walked slowly toward my inn, I met, in the shadow of a row of poplars, the garçon who had brought me my Burgundy a little time ago. I was thinking of Colonel Gaillarde, and I stopped the little waiter as he passed me.

"You said, I think, that Colonel Gaillarde was at the Belle Étoile for a week at one time."

"Yes, Monsieur."

"Is he perfectly in his right mind?"

The waiter stared. "Perfectly, Monsieur."

"Has he been suspected at any time of being out of his mind?"

"Never, Monsieur; he is a little noisy, but a very shrewd man."

"What is a fellow to think?" I muttered, as I walked on.

I was soon within sight of the lights of the Belle Étoile. A carriage, with four horses, stood in the moonlight at the door, and a furious altercation was going on in the hall, in which the yell of Colonel Gaillarde out-topped all other sounds.

Most young men like, at least, to witness a row. But, intuitively, I felt that this would interest me in a very special manner. I had only fifty yards to run, when I found myself in the hall of the old inn. The principal actor in this strange drama was, indeed, the Colonel, who stood facing the old Count de St. Alyre, who, in his traveling costume, with his black silk scarf covering the lower part of his face, confronted him; he had evidently been intercepted in an endeavor to reach his carriage. A little in the rear of the Count stood the Countess, also in traveling costume, with her thick black veil down, and holding in her delicate fingers a white rose. You can't conceive a more diabolical effigy of hate and fury than the Colonel; the knotted veins stood out on his forehead, his eyes were leaping from their sockets, he was grinding his teeth, and froth was on his lips. His sword was drawn in his hand, and he accompanied his yelling denunciations with stamps upon the floor and flourishes of his weapon in the air.

The host of the Belle Étoile was talking to the Colonel in soothing terms utterly thrown away. Two waiters, pale with fear, stared uselessly from behind. The Colonel screamed and thundered, and whirled his sword. "I was not sure of your red birds of prey; I could not believe you would have the audacity to travel on high roads, and to stop at honest inns, and lie under the same roof with honest men. You! *you! both—* vampires, wolves, ghouls. Summon the *gendarmes,* I say. By St. Peter and all the devils, if either of you try to get out of that door I'll take your heads off."

For a moment I had stood aghast. Here was a situation! I walked up to the lady; she laid her hand wildly upon my arm. "Oh! Monsieur," she whispered, in great agitation, “that dreadful madman! What are we to do? He won’t let us pass; he will kill my husband.”

“Fear nothing, Madame,” I answered, with romantic devotion, and stepping between the Count and Gaillarde, as he shrieked his invective, “Hold your tongue, and clear the way, you ruffian, you bully, you coward!” I roared.

A faint cry escaped the lady, which more than repaid the risk I ran, as the sword of the frantic soldier, after a moment’s astonished pause, flashed in the air to cut me down.

CHAPTER SEVEN

THE WHITE ROSE

I was too quick for Colonel Gaillarde. As he raised his sword, reckless of all consequences but my condign punishment and quite resolved to cleave me to the teeth, I struck him across the side of his head with my heavy stick, and while he staggered back I struck him another blow, nearly in the same place, that felled him to the floor, where he lay as if dead.

I did not care one of his own regimental buttons, whether he was dead or not; I was, at that moment, carried away by such a tumult of delightful and diabolical emotions!

I broke his sword under my foot, and flung the pieces across the street. The old Count de St. Alyre skipped nimbly without looking to the right or left, or thanking anybody, over the floor, out of the door, down the steps, and into his carriage. Instantly I was at the side of the beautiful Countess, thus left to shift for herself; I offered her my arm, which she took, and I led her to the carriage. She entered, and I shut the door. All this without a word.

I was about to ask if there were any commands with which she would honor me—my hand was laid upon the lower edge of the window, which was open.

The lady's hand was laid upon mine timidly and excitedly. Her lips almost touched my cheek as she whispered hurriedly:

"I may never see you more, and, oh! that I could forget you. Go—farewell—for God's sake, go!"

I pressed her hand for a moment. She withdrew it, but tremblingly pressed into mine the rose which she had held in her fingers during the agitating scene she had just passed through.

All this took place while the Count was commanding, entreating, cursing his servants, tipsy, and out of the way during the crisis, my conscience afterwards insinuated, by my clever contrivance. They now mounted to their places with the agility of alarm. The postilions' whips cracked, the horses scrambled into a trot, and away rolled the carriage, with its precious freightage, along the quaint main street, in the moonlight, toward Paris.

I stood on the pavement till it was quite lost to eye and ear in the distance.

With a deep sigh, I then turned, my white rose folded in my handkerchief—the little parting *gage*—the

Favor secret, sweet, and precious,

which no mortal eye but hers and mine had seen conveyed to me.

The care of the host of the Belle Étoile, and his assistants, had raised the wounded hero of a hundred fights partly against the wall, and propped him at each side with portmanteaus and pillows, and poured a glass of brandy, which was duly placed to his account, into his big mouth, where, for the first time, such a godsend remained unswallowed.

A bald-headed little military surgeon of sixty, with spectacles, who had cut off eighty-seven legs and arms to his own share, after the battle of Eylau, having retired with his sword and his saw, his laurels and his sticking-plaster to this, his native town, was called in, and rather thought the gallant Colonel's skull was fractured; at all events, there was concussion of the seat of thought, and quite enough work for his remarkable self-healing powers to occupy him for a fortnight.

I began to grow a little uneasy. A disagreeable surprise, if my excursion, in which I was to break banks and hearts, and, as you see, heads, should end upon the gallows or the guillotine. I was not clear, in those times of political oscillation, which was the established apparatus.

The Colonel was conveyed, snorting apoplectically, to his room.

I saw my host in the apartment in which we had supped. Wherever you employ a force of any sort, to carry a point of real importance, reject all nice calculations of economy. Better to be a thousand per cent, over the mark, than the smallest fraction of a unit under it. I instinctively felt this.

I ordered a bottle of my landlord's very best wine; made him partake with me, in the proportion of two glasses to one; and then told him that he must not decline a trifling *souvenir* from a guest who had been so charmed with all he had seen of the renowned Belle Étoile. Thus saying, I placed five-and-thirty Napoleons in his hand: at touch of which his countenance, by no means encouraging before, grew sunny, his manners thawed, and it was plain, as he dropped the coins hastily into his pocket, that benevolent relations had been established between us.

I immediately placed the Colonel's broken head upon the *tapis*. We both agreed that if I had not given him that rather smart tap of my walking-cane, he would have beheaded half the inmates of the Belle Étoile. There was not a waiter in the house who would not verify that statement on oath.

The reader may suppose that I had other motives, beside the desire to escape the tedious inquisition of the law, for desiring to recommence my journey to Paris with the least possible delay. Judge what was my horror then to learn that, for love or money, horses were nowhere to be had that night. The last pair in the town had been obtained from the Écu de France by a gentleman who dined and supped at the Belle Étoile, and was obliged to proceed to Paris that night.

Who was the gentleman? Had he actually gone? Could he possibly be induced to wait till morning?

The gentleman was now upstairs getting his things together, and his name was Monsieur Droqville.

I ran upstairs. I found my servant St. Clair in my room. At sight of him, for a moment, my thoughts were turned into a different channel.

"Well, St. Clair, tell me this moment who the lady is?" I demanded.

"The lady is the daughter or wife, it matters not which, of the Count de St. Alyre—the old gentleman who was so near being sliced like a cucumber tonight, I am informed, by the sword of the general whom Monsieur, by a turn of fortune, has put to bed of an apoplexy."

"Hold your tongue, fool! The man's beastly drunk—he's sulking—he could talk if he liked—who cares? Pack up my things. Which are Monsieur Droqville's apartments?"

He knew, of course; he always knew everything.

Half an hour later Monsieur Droqville and I were traveling towards Paris in my carriage and with his horses. I ventured to ask the Marquis d'Harmonville, in a little while, whether the lady, who accompanied the Count, was certainly the Countess. "Has he not a daughter?"

"Yes; I believe a very beautiful and charming young lady—I cannot say—it may have been she, his daughter by an earlier marriage. I saw only the Count himself today."

The Marquis was growing a little sleepy, and, in a little while, he actually fell asleep in his corner. I dozed and nodded; but the Marquis slept like a top. He awoke only for a minute or two at the next posting-house where he had fortunately secured horses by sending on his man, he told me. "You will excuse my being so dull a companion," he said, "but till tonight I have had but two hours' sleep, for more than sixty hours. I shall have a cup of coffee here; I have had my nap. Permit me to recommend you to do likewise. Their coffee is really excellent." He ordered two cups of *café noir,* and waited, with his head from the window. "We will keep the cups," he said, as he received them from the waiter, "and the tray. Thank you."

There was a little delay as he paid for these things; and then he took in the little tray, and handed me a cup of coffee.

I declined the tray; so he placed it on his own knees, to act as a miniature table.

"I can't endure being waited for and hurried," he said, "I like to sip my coffee at leisure."

I agreed. It really *was* the very perfection of coffee.

"I, like Monsieur le Marquis, have slept very little for the last two or three nights; and find it difficult to keep awake. This coffee will do wonders for me; it refreshes one so."

Before we had half done, the carriage was again in motion.

For a time our coffee made us chatty, and our conversation was animated.

The Marquis was extremely good-natured, as well as clever, and gave me a brilliant and amusing account of Parisian life, schemes, and dangers, all put so as to furnish me with practical warnings of the most valuable kind.

In spite of the amusing and curious stories which the Marquis related with so much point and color, I felt myself again becoming gradually drowsy and dreamy.

Perceiving this, no doubt, the Marquis good-naturedly suffered our conversation to subside into silence. The window next him was open. He threw his cup out of it; and did the same kind office for mine, and finally the little tray flew after, and I heard it clank on the road; a valuable waif, no doubt, for some early wayfarer in wooden shoes.

I leaned back in my corner; I had my beloved souvenir—my white rose—close to my heart, folded, now, in white paper. It inspired all manner of romantic dreams. I began to grow more and more sleepy. But actual slumber did not come. I was still viewing, with my half-closed eyes, from my corner, diagonally, the interior of the carriage.

I wished for sleep; but the barrier between waking and sleeping seemed absolutely insurmountable; and, instead, I entered into a state of novel and indescribable indolence.

The Marquis lifted his dispatch-box from the floor, placed it on his knees, unlocked it, and took out what proved to be a lamp, which he hung with two hooks, attached to it, to the window opposite to him. He lighted it with a match, put on his spectacles, and taking out a bundle of letters began to read them carefully.

We were making way very slowly. My impatience had hitherto employed four horses from stage to stage. We were in this emergency, only too happy to have secured two. But the difference in pace was depressing.

I grew tired of the monotony of seeing the spectacled Marquis reading, folding, and docketing, letter after letter. I wished to shut out the image which wearied me, but something prevented my being able to shut my eyes. I tried again and again; but, positively, I had lost the power of closing them.

I would have rubbed my eyes, but I could not stir my hand, my will no longer acted on my body—I found that I could not move one joint, or muscle, no more than I could, by an effort of my will, have turned the carriage about.

Up to this I had experienced no sense of horror. Whatever it was, simple nightmare was not the cause. I was awfully frightened! Was I in a fit?

It was horrible to see my good-natured companion pursue his occupation so serenely, when he might have dissipated my horrors by a single shake.

I made a stupendous exertion to call out, but in vain; I repeated the effort again and again, with no result.

My companion now tied up his letters, and looked out of the window, humming an air from an opera. He drew back his head, and said, turning to me:

"Yes, I see the lights; we shall be there in two or three minutes."

He looked more closely at me, and with a kind smile, and a little shrug, he said, "Poor child! how fatigued he must have been—how profoundly he sleeps! when the carriage stops he will waken."

He then replaced his letters in the box, locked it, put his spectacles in his pocket, and again looked out of the window.

We had entered a little town. I suppose it was past two o'clock by this time. The carriage drew up, I saw an inn-door open, and a light issuing from it.

"Here we are!" said my companion, turning gaily to me. But I did not awake.

"Yes, how tired he must have been!" he exclaimed, after he had waited for an answer. My servant was at the carriage door, and opened it.

"Your master sleeps soundly, he is so fatigued! It would be cruel to disturb him. You and I will go in, while they change the horses, and take some refreshment, and choose something that Monsieur Beckett will like to take in the carriage, for when he awakes by-and-by, he will, I am sure, be hungry."

He trimmed his lamp, poured in some oil; and taking care not to disturb me, with another kind smile and another word of caution to my servant he got out, and I heard him talking to St. Clair, as they entered the inn-door, and I was left in my corner, in the carriage, in the same state.

CHAPTER EIGHT

A THREE MINUTES' VISIT

I have suffered extreme and protracted bodily pain, at different periods of my life, but anything like that misery, thank God, I never endured before or since. I earnestly hope it may not resemble any type of death to which we are liable. I was, indeed, a spirit in prison; and unspeakable was my dumb and unmoving agony.

The power of thought remained clear and active. Dull terror filled my mind. How would this end? Was it actual death?

You will understand that my faculty of observing was unimpaired. I could hear and see anything as distinctly as ever I did in my life. It was simply that my will had, as it were, lost its hold of my body.

I told you that the Marquis d'Harmonville had not extinguished his carriage lamp on going into this village inn. I was listening intently, longing for his return, which might result, by some lucky accident, in awaking me from my catalepsy.

Without any sound of steps approaching, to announce an arrival, the carriage-door suddenly opened, and a total stranger got in silently and shut the door.

The lamp gave about as strong a light as a wax-candle, so I could see the intruder perfectly. He was a young man, with a dark grey loose surtout, made with a sort of hood, which was pulled over his head. I thought, as he moved, that I saw the gold band of a military undress cap under it; and I certainly saw the lace and buttons of a uniform, on the cuffs of the coat that were visible under the wide sleeves of his outside wrapper.

This young man had thick moustaches and an imperial, and I observed that he had a red scar running upward from his lip across his cheek.

He entered, shut the door softly, and sat down beside me. It was all done in a moment; leaning toward me, and shading his eyes with his gloved hand, he examined my face closely for a few seconds.

This man had come as noiselessly as a ghost; and everything he did was accomplished with the rapidity and decision that indicated a well-defined and pre-arranged plan. His designs were evidently sinister. I thought he was going to rob and, perhaps, murder me. I lay, nevertheless, like a corpse under his hands. He inserted his hand in my breast pocket, from which he took my precious white rose and all the letters it contained, among which was a paper of some consequence to me.

My letters he glanced at. They were plainly not what he wanted. My precious rose, too, he laid aside with them. It was evidently about the paper I have mentioned that he was concerned; for the moment he opened it he began with a pencil, in a small pocket-book, to make rapid notes of its contents.

This man seemed to glide through his work with a noiseless and cool celerity which argued, I thought, the training of the police department.

He rearranged the papers, possibly in the very order in which he had found them, replaced them in my breast-pocket, and was gone. His visit, I think, did not quite last three minutes. Very soon after his disappearance I heard the voice of the Marquis once more. He got in, and I saw him look at me and smile, half-envying me, I fancied, my sound repose. If he had but known all!

He resumed his reading and docketing by the light of the little lamp which had just subserved the purposes of a spy.

We were now out of the town, pursuing our journey at the same moderate pace. We had left the scene of my police visit, as I should have termed it, now two leagues behind us, when I suddenly felt a strange throbbing in one ear, and a sensation as if air passed through it into my throat. It seemed as if a bubble of air, formed deep in my ear, swelled, and burst there. The indescribable tension of my brain seemed all at once to give way; there was an odd humming in my head, and a sort of vibration through every nerve of my body, such as I have experienced in a limb that has been, in popular phraseology, asleep. I uttered a cry and half rose from my seat, and then fell back trembling, and with a sense of mortal faintness.

The Marquis stared at me, took my hand, and earnestly asked if I was ill. I could answer only with a deep groan.

Gradually the process of restoration was completed; and I was able, though very faintly, to tell him how very ill I had been; and then to describe the violation of my letters, during the time of his absence from the carriage.

"Good heaven!" he exclaimed, "the miscreant did not get at my box?"

I satisfied him, so far as I had observed, on that point. He placed the box on the seat beside him, and opened and examined its contents very minutely.

"Yes, undisturbed; all safe, thank heaven!" he murmured. "There are half-a-dozen letters here that I would not have some people read for a great deal."

He now asked with a very kind anxiety all about the illness I complained of. When he had heard me, he said:

"A friend of mine once had an attack as like yours as possible. It was on board ship, and followed a state of high excitement. He was a brave man like you; and was called on to exert both his strength and his courage suddenly. An hour or two after, fatigue overpowered him, and he appeared to fall into a sound sleep. He really sank into a state which he afterwards described so that I think it must have been precisely the same affection as yours."

"I am happy to think that my attack was not unique. Did he ever experience a return of it?"

"I knew him for years after, and never heard of any such thing. What strikes me is a parallel in the predisposing causes of each attack. Your unexpected and gallant hand-to-hand encounter, at such desperate odds, with an experienced swordsman, like that insane colonel of dragoons, your fatigue, and, finally, your composing yourself, as my other friend did, to sleep."

"I wish," he resumed, "one could make out who the *coquin* was who examined your letters. It is not worth turning back, however, because we should learn nothing. Those people always manage so adroitly. I am satisfied, however, that he must have been an agent of the police. A rogue of any other kind would have robbed you."

I talked very little, being ill and exhausted, but the Marquis talked on agreeably.

"We grow so intimate," said he, at last, "that I must remind you that I am not, for the present, the Marquis d'Harmonville, but only Monsieur Droqville; nevertheless, when we get to Paris, although I cannot see you often I may be of use. I shall ask you to name to me the hotel at which you mean to put up; because the Marquis being, as you are aware, on his travels, the Hotel d'Harmonville is, for the present, tenanted only by two or three old servants, who must not even see Monsieur Droqville. That gentleman will, nevertheless, contrive to get you access to the box of Monsieur le Marquis, at the Opera, as well, possibly, as to other places more difficult; and so soon as the diplomatic office of the Marquis d'Harmonville is ended, and he at liberty to declare himself, he will not excuse his friend, Monsieur Beckett, from fulfilling his promise to visit him this autumn at the Château d'Harmonville."

You may be sure I thanked the Marquis.

The nearer we got to Paris, the more I valued his protection. The countenance of a great man on the spot, just then, taking so kind an interest in the stranger whom he had, as it were, blundered upon, might make my visit ever so many degrees more delightful than I had anticipated.

Nothing could be more gracious than the manner and looks of the Marquis; and, as I still thanked him, the carriage suddenly stopped in front of the place where a relay of horses awaited us, and where, as it turned out, we were to part.

CHAPTER NINE

GOSSIP AND COUNSEL

My eventful journey was over at last. I sat in my hotel window looking out upon brilliant Paris, which had, in a moment, recovered all its gaiety, and more than its accustomed bustle. Everyone had read of the kind of excitement that followed the catastrophe of Napoleon, and the second restoration of the Bourbons. I need not, therefore, even if, at this distance, I could, recall and describe my experiences and impressions of the peculiar aspect of Paris, in those strange times. It was, to be sure, my first visit. But often as I have seen it since, I don't think I ever saw that delightful capital in a state, pleasurably so excited and exciting.

I had been two days in Paris, and had seen all sorts of sights, and experienced none of that rudeness and insolence of which others complained from the exasperated officers of the defeated French army.

I must say this, also. My romance had taken complete possession of me; and the chance of seeing the object of my dream gave a secret and delightful interest to my rambles and drives in the streets and environs, and my visits to the galleries and other sights of the metropolis.

I had neither seen nor heard of Count or Countess, nor had the Marquis d'Harmonville made any sign. I had quite recovered the strange indisposition under which I had suffered during my night journey.

It was now evening, and I was beginning to fear that my patrician acquaintance had quite forgotten me, when the waiter presented me the card of "Monsieur Droqville"; and, with no small elation and hurry, I desired him to show the gentleman up.

In came the Marquis d'Harmonville, kind and gracious as ever.

"I am a night-bird at present," said he, so soon as we had exchanged the little speeches which are usual. "I keep in the shade during the day-time, and even now I hardly ventured to come in a close carriage. The friends for whom I have undertaken a rather critical service, have so ordained it. They think all is lost if I am known to be in Paris. First, let me present you with these orders for my box. I am so vexed that I cannot command it oftener during the next fortnight; during my absence I had directed my secretary to give it for any night to the first of my friends who might apply, and the result is, that I find next to nothing left at my disposal."

I thanked him very much.

"And now a word in my office of Mentor. You have not come here, of course, without introductions?"

I produced half-a-dozen letters, the addresses of which he looked at.

"Don't mind these letters," he said. "I will introduce you. I will take you myself from house to house. One friend at your side is worth many letters. Make no intimacies, no acquaintances, until then. You young men like best to exhaust the public amusements of a great city, before embarrassing yourselves with the engagements of society. Go to all these. It will occupy you, day and night, for at least three weeks. When this is over, I shall be at liberty, and will myself introduce you to the brilliant but comparatively quiet routine of society. Place yourself in my hands; and in Paris remember, when once in society, you are always there."

I thanked him very much, and promised to follow his counsels implicitly. He seemed pleased, and said: "I shall now tell you some of the places you ought to go to. Take your map, and write letters or numbers upon the points I will indicate, and we will make out a little list. All the places that I shall mention to you are worth seeing."

In this methodical way, and with a great deal of amusing and scandalous anecdote, he furnished me with a catalogue and a guide, which, to a seeker of novelty and pleasure, was invaluable.

"In a fortnight, perhaps in a week," he said, "I shall be at leisure to be of real use to you. In the meantime, be on your guard. You must not play; you will be robbed if you do. Remember, you are surrounded, here, by plausible swindlers and villains of all kinds, who subsist by devouring strangers. Trust no one but those you know."

I thanked him again, and promised to profit by his advice. But my heart was too full of the beautiful lady of the Belle Étoile, to allow our interview to close without an effort to learn something about her. I therefore asked for the Count and Countess de St. Alyre, whom I had had the good fortune to extricate from an extremely unpleasant row in the hall of the inn.

Alas! he had not seen them since. He did not know where they were staying. They had a fine old house only a few leagues from Paris; but he thought it probable that they would remain, for a few days at least, in the city, as preparations would, no doubt, be necessary, after so long an absence, for their reception at home.

"How long have they been away?"

"About eight months, I think."

"They are poor, I think you said?"

"What *you* would consider poor. But, Monsieur, the Count has an income which affords them the comforts and even the elegancies of life, living as they do, in a very quiet and retired way, in this cheap country."

"Then they are very happy?"

"One would say they ought to be happy."

"And what prevents?"

"He is jealous."

"But his wife—she gives him no cause."

"I am afraid she does."

"How, Monsieur?"

"I always thought she was a little too—*a great deal* too—"

"Too *what,* Monsieur?"

"Too handsome. But although she has remarkable fine eyes, exquisite features, and the most delicate complexion in the world, I believe that she is a woman of probity. You have never seen her?"

"There was a lady, muffled up in a cloak, with a very thick veil on, the other night, in the hall of the Belle Étoile, when I broke that fellow's head who was bullying the old Count. But her veil was so thick I could not see a feature through it!" My answer was diplomatic, you observe. "She may have been the Count's daughter. Do they quarrel?"

"Who, he and his wife?"

"Yes."

"A little."

"Oh! and what do they quarrel about?"

"It is a long story; about the lady's diamonds. They are valuable—they are worth, La Perelleuse says, about a million of francs. The Count wishes them sold and turned into revenue, which he offers to settle as she pleases. The Countess, whose they are, resists, and for a reason which, I rather think, she can't disclose to him."

"And pray what is that?" I asked, my curiosity a good deal piqued.

"She is thinking, I conjecture, how well she will look in them when she marries her second husband."

"Oh?—yes, to be sure. But the Count de St. Alyre is a good man?"

"Admirable, and extremely intelligent."

"I should wish so much to be presented to the Count: you tell me he's so—"

"So agreeably married. But they are living quite out of the world. He takes her now and then to the Opera, or to a public entertainment; but that is all."

"And he must remember so much of the old *régime,* and so many of the scenes of the revolution!"

"Yes, the very man for a philosopher, like you! And he falls asleep after dinner; and his wife don't. But, seriously, he has retired from the gay and the great world, and has grown apathetic; and so has his wife; and nothing seems to interest her now, not even—her husband!"

The Marquis stood up to take his leave.

"Don't risk your money," said he. "You will soon have an opportunity of laying out some of it to great advantage. Several collections of really good pictures, belonging to persons who have mixed themselves up in this Bonapartist restoration, must come within a few weeks to the hammer. You can do wonders when these sales commence. There will be startling bargains! Reserve yourself for them. I shall let you know all about it. By-the-by," he said, stopping short as he approached the door, "I was so near forgetting. There is to be next week, the very thing you would enjoy so much, because you see so little of it in England—I mean a *bal masqué,* conducted, it is said, with more than usual splendor. It takes place at Versailles—all the world will be there; there is such a rush for cards! But I think I may promise you one. Good-night! Adieu!"

CHAPTER TEN

THE BLACK VEIL

Speaking the language fluently, and with unlimited money, there was nothing to prevent my enjoying all that was enjoyable in the French capital. You may easily suppose how two days were passed. At the end of that time, and at about the same hour, Monsieur Droqville called again.

Courtly, good-natured, gay, as usual, he told me that the masquerade ball was fixed for the next Wednesday, and that he had applied for a card for me.

How awfully unlucky. I was so afraid I should not be able to go.

He stared at me for a moment with a suspicious and menacing look, which I did not understand, in silence, and then inquired rather sharply. And will Monsieur Beckett be good enough to say why not?

I was a little surprised, but answered the simple truth: I had made an engagement for that evening with two or three English friends, and did not see how I could.

"Just so! You English, wherever you are, always look out for your English boors, your beer and bifstek; and when you come here, instead of trying to learn something of the people you visit, and pretend to study, you are guzzling and swearing, and smoking with one another, and no wiser or more polished at the end of your travels than if you had been all the time carousing in a booth at Greenwich."

He laughed sarcastically, and looked as if he could have poisoned me.

"There it is," said he, throwing the card on the table. "Take it or leave it, just as you please. I suppose I shall have my trouble for my pains; but it is not usual when a man such as I takes trouble, asks a favor, and secures a privilege for an acquaintance, to treat him so."

This was astonishingly impertinent.

I was shocked, offended, penitent. I had possibly committed unwittingly a breach of good breeding, according to French ideas, which almost justified the brusque severity of the Marquis's undignified rebuke.

In a confusion, therefore, of many feelings, I hastened to make my apologies, and to propitiate the chance friend who had showed me so much disinterested kindness.

I told him that I would, at any cost, break through the engagement in which I had unluckily entangled myself; that I had spoken with too little reflection, and that I certainly had not thanked him at all in proportion to his kindness, and to my real estimate of it.

"Pray say not a word more; my vexation was entirely on your account; and I expressed it, I am only too conscious, in terms a great deal too strong, which, I am sure, your good nature will pardon. Those who know me a little better are aware that I sometimes say a good deal more than I intend; and am always sorry when I do. Monsieur Beckett will forget that his old friend Monsieur Droqville has lost his temper in his cause, for a moment, and—we are as good friends as before."

He smiled like the Monsieur Droqville of the Belle Étoile, and extended his hand, which I took very respectfully and cordially.

Our momentary quarrel had left us only better friends.

The Marquis then told me I had better secure a bed in some hotel at Versailles, as a rush would be made to take them; and advised my going down next morning for the purpose.

I ordered horses accordingly for eleven o'clock; and, after a little more conversation, the Marquis d'Harmonville bade me good-night, and ran down the stairs with his handkerchief to his mouth and nose, and, as

I saw from my window, jumped into his close carriage again and drove away.

Next day I was at Versailles. As I approached the door of the Hotel de France it was plain that I was not a moment too soon, if, indeed, I were not already too late.

A crowd of carriages were drawn up about the entrance, so that I had no chance of approaching except by dismounting and pushing my way among the horses. The hall was full of servants and gentlemen screaming to the proprietor, who in a state of polite distraction was assuring them, one and all, that there was not a room or a closet disengaged in his entire house.

I slipped out again, leaving the hall to those who were shouting, expostulating, and wheedling, in the delusion that the host might, if he pleased, manage something for them. I jumped into my carriage and drove, at my horses' best pace, to the Hotel du Reservoir. The blockade about this door was as complete as the other. The result was the same. It was very provoking, but what was to be done? My postilion had, a little officiously, while I was in the hall talking with the hotel authorities, got his horses, bit by bit, as other carriages moved away, to the very steps of the inn door.

This arrangement was very convenient so far as getting in again was concerned. But, this accomplished, how were we to get on? There were carriages in front, and carriages behind, and no less than four rows of carriages, of all sorts, outside.

I had at this time remarkably long and clear sight, and if I had been impatient before, guess what my feelings were when I saw an open carriage pass along the narrow strip of roadway left open at the other side, a barouche in which I was certain I recognized the veiled Countess and her husband. This carriage had been brought to a walk by a cart which occupied the whole breadth of the narrow way, and was moving with the customary tardiness of such vehicles.

I should have done more wisely if I had jumped down on the *trottoir*, and run round the block of carriages in front of the barouche. But, unfortunately, I was more of a Murat than a Moltke, and preferred a direct charge upon my object to relying on *tactique*. I dashed across the back seat of a carriage which was next mine, I don't know how; tumbled through a sort of gig, in which an old gentleman and a dog were dozing; stepped with an incoherent apology over the side of an open carriage, in which were four gentlemen engaged in a hot dispute; tripped at the far side in getting out, and fell flat across the backs of a pair of horses, who instantly began plunging and threw me head foremost in the dust.

To those who observed my reckless charge, without being in the secret of my object, I must have appeared demented. Fortunately, the interesting barouche had passed before the catastrophe, and covered as I was with dust, and my hat blocked, you may be sure I did not care to present myself before the object of my Quixotic devotion.

I stood for a while amid a storm of *sacré*-ing, tempered disagreeably with laughter; and in the midst of these, while endeavoring to beat the dust from my clothes with my handkerchief, I heard a voice with which I was acquainted call, "Monsieur Beckett."

I looked and saw the Marquis peeping from a carriage-window. It was a welcome sight. In a moment I was at his carriage side.

"You may as well leave Versailles," he said; "you have learned, no doubt, that there is not a bed to hire in either of the hotels; and I can add that there is not a room to let in the whole town. But I have managed something for you that will answer just as well. Tell your servant to follow us, and get in here and sit beside me."

Fortunately an opening in the closely packed carriages had just occurred, and mine was approaching.

I directed the servant to follow us; and the Marquis having said a word to his driver, we were immediately in motion.

"I will bring you to a comfortable place, the very existence of which is known to but few Parisians, where, knowing how things were here, I secured a room for you. It is only a mile away, and an old comfortable inn, called the Le Dragon Volant. It was fortunate for you that my tiresome business called me to this place so early."

I think we had driven about a mile-and-a-half to the further side of the palace when we found ourselves upon a narrow old road, with the woods of Versailles on one side, and much older trees, of a size seldom seen in France, on the other.

We pulled up before an antique and solid inn, built of Caen stone, in a fashion richer and more florid than was ever usual in such houses, and which indicated that it was originally designed for the private mansion of some person of wealth, and probably, as the wall bore many carved shields and supporters, of distinction also. A kind of porch, less ancient than the rest, projected hospitably with a wide and florid arch, over which, cut in high relief in stone, and painted and gilded, was the sign of the inn. This was the Flying Dragon, with wings of brilliant red and gold, expanded, and its tail, pale green and gold, twisted and knotted into ever so many rings, and ending in a burnished point barbed like the dart of death.

"I shan't go in—but you will find it a comfortable place; at all events better than nothing. I would go in with you, but my incognito forbids. You will, I daresay, be all the better pleased to learn that the inn is haunted—I should have been, in my young days, I know. But don't allude to that awful fact in hearing of your host, for I believe it is a sore subject. Adieu. If you want to enjoy yourself at the ball, take my advice and go in a domino. I think I shall look in; and certainly, if I do, in the same costume. How shall we recognize one another? Let me see, something held in the fingers—a flower won't do, so many people will have flowers. Suppose you get a red cross a couple of inches long— you're an Englishman—stitched or pinned on the breast of your domino, and I a white one? Yes, that will do very well; and whatever room you go into keep near the door till we meet. I shall look for you at all the doors I pass; and you, in the same way, for me; and we *must* find each other soon. So that is understood. I can't enjoy a thing of that kind with any but a young person; a man of my age requires the contagion of young spirits and the companionship of someone who enjoys everything spontaneously. Farewell; we meet tonight."

By this time I was standing on the road; I shut the carriage-door; bid him good-bye; and away he drove.

CHAPTER ELEVEN

THE DRAGON VOLANT

I took one look about me.

The building was picturesque; the trees made it more so. The antique and sequestered character of the scene contrasted strangely with the glare and bustle of the Parisian life, to which my eye and ear had become accustomed.

Then I examined the gorgeous old sign for a minute or two. Next I surveyed the exterior of the house more carefully. It was large and solid, and squared more with my ideas of an ancient English hostelrie, such as the Canterbury Pilgrims might have put up at, than a French house of entertainment. Except, indeed, for a round turret, that rose at the left flank of the house, and terminated in the extinguisher-shaped roof that suggests a French château.

I entered and announced myself as Monsieur Beckett, for whom a room had been taken. I was received with all the consideration due to an English milord, with, of course, an unfathomable purse.

My host conducted me to my apartment. It was a large room, a little somber, paneled with dark wainscoting, and furnished in a stately and somber style, long out of date. There was a wide hearth, and a heavy mantelpiece, carved with shields, in which I might, had I been curious enough, have discovered a correspondence with the heraldry on the outer walls. There was something interesting, melancholy, and even depressing in all this. I went to the stone-shafted window, and looked out upon a small park, with a thick wood, forming the background of a château which presented a cluster of such conical-topped turrets as I have just now mentioned.

The wood and château were melancholy objects. They showed signs of neglect, and almost of decay; and the gloom of fallen grandeur, and a certain air of desertion hung oppressively over the scene.

I asked my host the name of the château.

"That, Monsieur, is the Château de la Carque," he answered.

"It is a pity it is so neglected," I observed. "I should say, perhaps, a pity that its proprietor is not more wealthy?"

"Perhaps so, Monsieur."

"*Perhaps?*" I repeated, and looked at him. "Then I suppose he is not very popular."

"Neither one thing nor the other, Monsieur," he answered; "I meant only that we could not tell what use he might make of riches."

"And who is he?" I inquired.

"The Count de St. Alyre."

"Oh! The Count! You are quite sure?" I asked, very eagerly.

It was now the innkeeper's turn to look at me.

"*Quite* sure, Monsieur, the Count de St. Alyre."

"Do you see much of him in this part of the world?"

"Not a great deal, Monsieur; he is often absent for a considerable time."

"And is he poor?" I inquired.

"I pay rent to him for this house. It is not much; but I find he cannot wait long for it," he replied, smiling satirically.

"From what I have heard, however, I should think he cannot be very poor?" I continued.

"They say, Monsieur, he plays. I know not. He certainly is not rich. About seven months ago, a relation of his died in a distant place. His body was sent to the Count's house here, and by him buried in Père la

Chaise, as the poor gentleman had desired. The Count was in profound affliction; although he got a handsome legacy, they say, by that death. But money never seems to do him good for any time."

"He is old, I believe?"

"Old? We call him the 'Wandering Jew,' except, indeed, that he has not always the five sous in his pocket. Yet, Monsieur, his courage does not fail him. He has taken a young and handsome wife."

"And she?" I urged—

"Is the Countess de St. Alyre."

"Yes; but I fancy we may say something more? She has attributes?"

"Three, Monsieur, three, at least most amiable."

"Ah! And what are they?"

"Youth, beauty, and—diamonds."

I laughed. The sly old gentleman was foiling my curiosity.

"I see, my friend," said I, "you are reluctant—"

"To quarrel with the Count," he concluded. "True. You see, Monsieur, he could vex me in two or three ways, so could I him. But, on the whole, it is better each to mind his business, and to maintain peaceful relations; you understand."

It was, therefore, no use trying, at least for the present. Perhaps he had nothing to relate. Should I think differently, by-and-by, I could try the effect of a few Napoleons. Possibly he meant to extract them.

The host of the Dragon Volant was an elderly man, thin, bronzed, intelligent, and with an air of decision, perfectly military. I learned afterwards that he had served under Napoleon in his early Italian campaigns.

"One question, I think you may answer," I said, "without risking a quarrel. Is the Count at home?"

"He has many homes, I conjecture," said the host evasively. "But—but I think I may say, Monsieur, that he is, I believe, at present staying at the Château de la Carque."

I looked out of the window, more interested than ever, across the undulating grounds to the château, with its gloomy background of foliage.

"I saw him today, in his carriage at Versailles," I said.

"Very natural."

"Then his carriage, and horses, and servants, are at the château?"

"The carriage he puts up here, Monsieur, and the servants are hired for the occasion. There is but one who sleeps at the château. Such a life must be terrifying for Madame the Countess," he replied.

"The old screw!" I thought. "By this torture, he hopes to extract her diamonds. What a life! What fiends to contend with—jealousy and extortion!"

The knight having made his speech to himself, cast his eyes once more upon the enchanter's castle, and heaved a gentle sigh—a sigh of longing, of resolution, and of love.

What a fool I was! And yet, in the sight of angels, are we any wiser as we grow older? It seems to me, only, that our illusions change as we go on; but, still, we are madmen all the same.

"Well, St. Clair," said I, as my servant entered, and began to arrange my things.

"You have got a bed?"

"In the cock-loft, Monsieur, among the spiders, and, *par ma foi*! the cats and the owls. But we agree very well. *Vive la bagatelle*!"

"I had no idea it was so full."

"Chiefly the servants, Monsieur, of those persons who were fortunate enough to get apartments at Versailles."

"And what do you think of the Dragon Volant?"

"The Dragon Volant! Monsieur; the old fiery dragon! The devil himself, if all is true! On the faith of a Christian, Monsieur, they say that diabolical miracles have taken place in this house."

"What do you mean? *Revenants*?"

"Not at all, sir; I wish it was no worse. *Revenants*? No! People who have never returned—who vanished, before the eyes of half-a-dozen men all looking at them."

"What do you mean, St. Clair? Let us hear the story, or miracle, or whatever it is."

"It is only this, Monsieur, that an ex-master-of-the-horse of the late king, who lost his head—Monsieur will have the goodness to recollect, in the revolution—being permitted by the Emperor to return to France, lived here in this hotel, for a month, and at the end of that time vanished, visibly, as I told you, before the faces of half-a-dozen credible witnesses! The other was a Russian nobleman, six feet high and upwards, who, standing in the center of the room, downstairs, describing to seven gentlemen of unquestionable veracity the last moments of Peter the Great, and having a glass of *eau de vie* in his left hand, and his *tasse de cafe*, nearly finished, in his right, in like manner vanished. His boots were found on the floor where he had been standing; and the gentleman at his right found, to his astonishment, his cup of coffee in his fingers, and the gentleman at his left, his glass of *eau de vie*—"

"Which he swallowed in his confusion," I suggested.

"Which was preserved for three years among the curious articles of this house, and was broken by the *curé* while conversing with Mademoiselle Fidone in the housekeeper's room; but of the Russian nobleman himself, nothing more was ever seen or heard. *Parbleu*! when *we* go out of the Dragon Volant, I hope it may be by the door. I heard all this, Monsieur, from the postilion who drove us."

"Then it *must* be true!" said I, jocularly: but I was beginning to feel the gloom of the view, and of the chamber in which I stood; there had stolen over me, I know not how, a presentiment of evil; and my joke was with an effort, and my spirit flagged.

CHAPTER TWELVE

THE MAGICIAN

No more brilliant spectacle than this masked ball could be imagined. Among other *salons* and galleries, thrown open, was the enormous Perspective of the "Grande Galerie des Glaces," lighted up on that occasion with no less than four thousand wax candles, reflected and repeated by all the mirrors, so that the effect was almost dazzling. The grand suite of *salons* was thronged with masques, in every conceivable costume. There was not a single room deserted. Everyplace was animated with music voices, brilliant colors, flashing jewels, the hilarity of extemporized comedy, and all the spirited incidents of a cleverly sustained masquerade. I had never seen before anything in the least comparable to this magnificent *fete.* I moved along, indolently, in my domino and mask, loitering, now and then, to enjoy a clever dialogue, a farcical song, or an amusing monologue, but, at the same time, keeping my eyes about me, lest my friend in the black domino, with the little white cross on his breast, should pass me by.

I had delayed and looked about me, specially, at every door I passed, as the Marquis and I had agreed; but he had not yet appeared.

While I was thus employed, in the very luxury of lazy amusement, I saw a gilded sedan chair, or, rather, a Chinese palanquin, exhibiting the fantastic exuberance of "Celestial" decoration, borne forward on gilded poles by four richly dressed Chinese; one with a wand in his hand marched in front, and another behind; and a slight and solemn man, with a long black beard, a tall fez, such as a dervish is represented as wearing, walked close to its side. A strangely embroidered robe fell over his shoulders, covered with hieroglyphic symbols; the embroidery was in black and gold, upon a variegated ground of brilliant colors. The robe was bound about his waist with a broad belt of gold, with cabalistic devices traced on it in dark red and black; red stockings, and shoes embroidered with gold, and pointed and curved upward at the toes, in Oriental fashion, appeared below the skirt of the robe. The man's face was dark, fixed, and solemn, and his eyebrows black, and enormously heavy—he carried a singular-looking book under his arm, a wand of polished black wood in his other hand, and walked with his chin sunk on his breast, and his eyes fixed upon the floor. The man in front waved his wand right and left to clear the .way for the advancing palanquin, the curtains of which were closed; and there was something so singular, strange and solemn about the whole thing, that I felt at once interested.

I was very well pleased when I saw the bearers set down their burthen within a few yards of the spot on which I stood.

The bearers and the men with the gilded wands forthwith clapped their hands, and in silence danced round the palanquin a curious and half-frantic dance, which was yet, as to figures and postures, perfectly methodical. This was soon accompanied by a clapping of hands and a ha-ha-ing, rhythmically delivered.

While the dance was going on a hand was lightly laid on my arm, and, looking round, a black domino with a white cross stood beside me.

"I am so glad I have found you," said the Marquis; "and at this moment. This is the best group in the rooms. *You* must speak to the wizard. About an hour ago I lighted upon them, in another *salon*, and consulted the oracle by putting questions. I never was more amazed. Although his answers were a little disguised it was soon perfectly plain that he knew every detail about the business, which no one on earth had heard of but myself, and two or three other men, about the most cautious persons in

France. I shall never forget that shock. I saw other people who consulted him, evidently as much surprised and more frightened than I. I came with the Count de St. Alyre and the Countess."

He nodded toward a thin figure, also in a domino. It was the Count.

"Come," he said to me, "I'll introduce you."

I followed, you may suppose, readily enough.

The Marquis presented me, with a very prettily-turned allusion to my fortunate intervention in his favor at the Belle Étoile; and the Count overwhelmed me with polite speeches, and ended by saying, what pleased me better still:

"The Countess is near us, in the next salon but one, chatting with her old friend the Duchesse d'Argensaque; I shall go for her in a few minutes; and when I bring her here, she shall make your acquaintance; and thank you, also, for your assistance, rendered with so much courage when we were so very disagreeably interrupted."

"You must, positively, speak with the magician," said the Marquis to the Count de St. Alyre, "you will be so much amused. *I* did so; and, I assure you, I could not have anticipated such answers! I don't know what to believe."

"Really! Then, by all means, let us try," he replied.

We three approached, together, the side of the palanquin, at which the black-bearded magician stood.

A young man, in a Spanish dress, who, with a friend at his side, had just conferred with the conjuror, was saying, as he passed us by:

"Ingenious mystification! Who is that in the palanquin? He seems to know everybody!"

The Count, in his mask and domino, moved along, stiffly, with us, toward the palanquin. A clear circle was maintained by the Chinese attendants, and the spectators crowded round in a ring.

One of these men—he who with a gilded wand had preceded the procession—advanced, extending his empty hand, palm upward.

"Money?" inquired the Count.

"Gold," replied the usher.

The Count placed a piece of money in his hand; and I and the Marquis were each called on in turn to do likewise as we entered the circle. We paid accordingly.

The conjuror stood beside the palanquin, its silk curtain in his hand; his chin sunk, with its long, jet-black beard, on his chest; the outer hand grasping the black wand, on which he leaned; his eyes were lowered, as before, to the ground; his face looked absolutely lifeless. Indeed, I never saw face or figure so moveless, except in death. The first question the Count put, was: "Am I married, or unmarried?"

The conjuror drew back the curtain quickly, and placed his ear toward a richly-dressed Chinese, who sat in the litter; withdrew his head, and closed the curtain again; and then answered: "Yes."

The same preliminary was observed each time, so that the man with the black wand presented himself, not as a prophet, but as a medium; and answered, as it seemed, in the words of a greater than himself.

Two or three questions followed, the answers to which seemed to amuse the Marquis very much; but the point of which I could not see, for I knew next to nothing of the Count's peculiarities and adventures.

"Does my wife love me?" asked he, playfully.

"As well as you deserve."

"Whom do I love best in the world?"

"Self."

"Oh! That I fancy is pretty much the case with everyone. But, putting myself out of the question, do I love anything on earth better than my wife?"

"Her diamonds."

"Oh!" said the Count. The Marquis, I could see, laughed.

"Is it true," said the Count, changing the conversation peremptorily, "that there has been a battle in Naples?"

"No; in France."

"Indeed," said the Count, satirically, with a glance round.

"And may I inquire between what powers, and on what particular quarrel?"

"Between the Count and Countess de St. Alyre, and about a document they subscribed on the 25th July, 1811."

The Marquis afterwards told me that this was the date of their marriage settlement.

The Count stood stock-still for a minute or so; and one could fancy that they saw his face flushing through his mask.

Nobody, but we two, knew that the inquirer was the Count de St. Alyre.

I thought he was puzzled to find a subject for his next question; and, perhaps, repented having entangled himself in such a colloquy. If so, he was relieved; for the Marquis, touching his arms, whispered.

"Look to your right, and see who is coming."

I looked in the direction indicated by the Marquis, and I saw a gaunt figure stalking toward us. It was not a masque. The face was broad, scarred, and white. In a word, it was the ugly face of Colonel Gaillarde, who, in the costume of a corporal of the Imperial Guard, with his left arm so adjusted as to look like a stump, leaving the lower part of the coat-sleeve empty, and pinned up to the breast. There were strips of very real sticking-plaster across his eyebrow and temple, where my stick had left its mark, to score, hereafter, among the more honorable scars of war.

CHAPTER THIRTEEN

THE ORACLE TELLS ME WONDERS

I forgot for a moment how impervious my mask and domino were to the hard stare of the old campaigner, and was preparing for an animated scuffle. It was only for a moment, of course; but the count cautiously drew a little back as the gasconading corporal, in blue uniform, white vest, and white gaiters—for my friend Gaillarde was as loud and swaggering in his assumed character as in his real one of a colonel of dragoons—drew near. He had already twice all but got himself turned out of doors for vaunting the exploits of Napoleon le Grand, in terrific mock-heroics, and had very nearly come to hand-grips with a Prussian hussar. In fact, he would have been involved in several sanguinary rows already, had not his discretion reminded him that the object of his coming there at all, namely, to arrange a meeting with an affluent widow, on whom he believed he had made a tender impression, would not have been promoted by his premature removal from the festive scene of which he was an ornament, in charge of a couple of *gendarmes.*

"Money! Gold! Bah! What money can a wounded soldier like your humble servant have amassed, with but his sword-hand left, which, being necessarily occupied, places not a finger at his command with which to scrape together the spoils of a routed enemy?"

"No gold from him," said the magician. "His scars frank him."

"Bravo, Monsieur le prophète! Bravissimo! Here I am. Shall I begin, *mon sorcier*, without further loss of time, to question you?"

Without waiting for an answer, he commenced, in stentorian tones. After half-a-dozen questions and answers, he asked: "Whom do I pursue at present?"

"Two persons."

"Ha! Two? Well, who are they?"

"An Englishman, whom if you catch, he will kill you; and a French widow, whom if you find, she will spit in your face."

"Monsieur le magicien calls a spade a spade, and knows that his cloth protects him. No matter! Why do I pursue them?"

"The widow has inflicted a wound on your heart, and the Englishman a wound on your head. They are each separately too strong for you; take care your pursuit does not unite them."

"Bah! How could that be?"

"The Englishman protects ladies. He has got that fact into your head. The widow, if she sees, will marry him. It takes some time, she will reflect, to become a colonel, and the Englishman is unquestionably young."

"I will cut his cock's-comb for him," he ejaculated with an oath and a grin; and in a softer tone he asked, "Where is she?"

"Near enough to be offended if you fail."

"So she ought, by my faith. You are right, Monsieur le prophète! A hundred thousand thanks! Farewell!" And staring about him, and stretching his lank neck as high as he could, he strode away with his scars, and white waistcoat and gaiters, and his bearskin shako.

I had been trying to see the person who sat in the palanquin. I had only once an opportunity of a tolerably steady peep. What I saw was singular. The oracle was dressed, as I have said, very richly, in the Chinese fashion. He was a figure altogether on a larger scale than the interpreter, who stood outside. The features seemed to me large and heavy, and the head was carried with a downward inclination! The eyes were closed, and the chin rested on the breast of his embroidered pelisse. The face seemed fixed, and the very image of apathy. Its character and *pose* seemed an exaggerated repetition of the immobility of the figure who communicated with the noisy outer world. This face looked blood-red; but that was caused, I concluded, by the light entering through the red silk curtains. All this struck me almost at a glance; I had not many seconds in which to make my observation. The ground was now clear, and the Marquis said, "Go forward, my friend."

I did so. When I reached the magician, as we called the man with the black wand, I glanced over my shoulder to see whether the Count was near.

No, he was some yards behind; and he and the Marquis, whose curiosity seemed to be by this time satisfied, were now conversing generally upon some subject of course quite different.

I was relieved, for the sage seemed to blurt out secrets in an unexpected way; and some of mine might not have amused the Count.

I thought for a moment. I wished to test the prophet. A Church-of-England man was a *rara avis* in Paris.

"What is my religion?" I asked.

"A beautiful heresy," answered the oracle instantly.

"A heresy?—and pray how is it named?"

"Love."

"Oh! Then I suppose I am a polytheist, and love a great many?"

"One."

"But, seriously," I asked, intending to turn the course of our colloquy a little out of an embarrassing channel, "have I ever learned any words of devotion by heart?"

"Yes."

"Can you repeat them?"

"Approach."

I did, and lowered my ear.

The man with the black wand closed the curtains, and whispered, slowly and distinctly, these words which, I need scarcely tell you, I instantly recognized:

"I may never see you more; and, oh! I that I could forget you!—go—farewell—for God's sake, go!"

I started as I heard them. They were, you know, the last words whispered to me by the Countess.

"Good Heavens! How miraculous! Words heard most assuredly, by no ear on earth but my own and the lady's who uttered them, till now!"

I looked at the impassive face of the spokesman with the wand. There was no trace of meaning, or even of a consciousness that the words he had uttered could possibly interest me.

"What do I most long for?" I asked, scarcely knowing what I said.

"Paradise."

"And what prevents my reaching it?"

"A black veil."

Stronger and stronger! The answers seemed to me to indicate the minutest acquaintance with every detail of my little romance, of which not even the Marquis knew anything! And I, the questioner, masked and robed so that my own brother could not have known me!

"You said I loved someone. Am I loved in return?" I asked.

"Try."

I was speaking lower than before, and stood near the dark man with the beard, to prevent the necessity of his speaking in a loud key.

"Does anyone love me?" I repeated.

"Secretly," was the answer.

"Much or little?" I inquired.

"Too well."

"How long will that love last?"

"Till the rose casts its leaves."

The rose—another allusion!

"Then—darkness!" I sighed. "But till then I live in light."

"The light of violet eyes."

Love, if not a religion, as the oracle had just pronounced it, is, at least, a superstition. How it exalts the imagination! How it enervates the reason! How credulous it makes us!

All this which, in the case of another I should have laughed at, most powerfully affected me in my own. It inflamed my ardor, and half crazed my brain, and even influenced my conduct.

The spokesman of this wonderful trick—if trick it were—now waved me backward with his wand, and as I withdrew, my eyes still fixed upon the group, and this time encircled with an aura of mystery in my fancy; backing toward the ring of spectators, I saw him raise his hand suddenly, with a gesture of command, as a signal to the usher who carried the golden wand in front.

The usher struck his wand on the ground, and, in a shrill voice, proclaimed: "The great Confu is silent for an hour."

Instantly the bearers pulled down a sort of blind of bamboo, which descended with a sharp clatter, and secured it at the bottom; and then the man in the tall fez, with the black beard and wand, began a sort of dervish dance. In this the men with the gold wands joined, and finally, in an outer ring, the bearers, the palanquin being the center of the circles described by these solemn dancers, whose pace, little by little, quickened, whose gestures grew sudden, strange, frantic, as the motion became swifter and swifter, until at length the whirl became so rapid that the dancers seemed to fly by with the speed of a mill-wheel, and amid a general clapping of hands, and universal wonder, these strange performers mingled with the crowd, and the exhibition, for the time at least, ended.

The Marquis d'Harmonville was standing not far away, looking on the ground, as one could judge by his attitude and musing. I approached, and he said:

"The Count has just gone away to look for his wife. It is a pity she was not here to consult the prophet; it would have been amusing, I daresay, to see how the Count bore it. Suppose we follow him. I have asked him to introduce you."

With a beating heart, I accompanied the Marquis d'Harmonville.

CHAPTER FOURTEEN

MADEMOISELLE DE LA VALLIÈRE

We wandered through the *salons*, the Marquis and I. It was no easy matter to find a friend in rooms so crowded.

"Stay here," said the Marquis, "I have thought of a way of finding him. Besides, his jealousy may have warned him that there is no particular advantage to be gained by presenting you to his wife; I had better go and reason with him, as you seem to wish an introduction so very much."

This occurred in the room that is now called the "Salon d'Apollon." The paintings remained in my memory, and my adventure of that evening was destined to occur there.

I sat down upon a sofa, and looked about me. Three or four persons beside myself were seated on this roomy piece of gilded furniture. They were chatting all very gaily; all—except the person who sat next me, and she was a lady. Hardly two feet interposed between us. The lady sat apparently in a reverie. Nothing could be more graceful. She wore the costume perpetuated in Collignan's full-length portrait of Mademoiselle de la Valière. It is, as you know, not only rich, but elegant. Her hair was powdered, but one could perceive that it was naturally a dark brown. One pretty little foot appeared, and could anything be more exquisite than her hand?

It was extremely provoking that this lady wore her mask, and did not, as many did, hold it for a time in her hand.

I was convinced that she was pretty. Availing myself of the privilege of a masquerade, a microcosm in which it is impossible, except by voice and allusion, to distinguish friend from foe, I spoke:

"It is not easy, Mademoiselle, to deceive me," I began.

"So much the better for Monsieur," answered the mask, quietly.

"I mean," I said, determined to tell my fib, "that beauty is a gift more difficult to conceal than Mademoiselle supposes."

"Yet Monsieur has succeeded very well," she said in the same sweet and careless tones.

"I see the costume of this, the beautiful Mademoiselle de la Valière, upon a form that surpasses her own; I raise my eyes, and I behold a mask, and yet I recognize the lady; beauty is like that precious stone in the 'Arabian Nights,' which emits, no matter how concealed, a light that betrays it."

"I know the story," said the young lady. "The light betrayed it, not in the sun but in darkness. Is there so little light in these rooms, Monsieur, that a poor glowworm can show so brightly? I thought we were in a luminous atmosphere, wherever a certain Countess moved?"

Here was an awkward speech! How was I to answer? This lady might be, as they say some ladies are, a lover of mischief, or an intimate of the Countess de St. Alyre. Cautiously, therefore, I inquired,

"What Countess?"

"If you know me, you must know that she is my dearest friend. Is she not beautiful?"

"How can I answer, there are so many countesses."

"Everyone who knows me, knows who my best beloved friend is. You don't know me?"

"That is cruel. I can scarcely believe I am mistaken."

"With whom were you walking, just now?" she asked.

"A gentleman, a friend," I answered.

"I saw him, of course, a friend; but I think I know him, and should like to be certain. Is he not a certain Marquis?"

Here was another question that was extremely awkward.

"There are so many people here, and one may walk, at one time with one, and at another with a different one, that—"

"That an unscrupulous person has no difficulty in evading a simple question like mine. Know then, once for all, that nothing disgusts a person of spirit so much as suspicion. You, Monsieur, are a gentleman of discretion. I shall respect you accordingly."

"Mademoiselle would despise me, were I to violate a confidence."

"But you don't deceive me. You imitate your friend's diplomacy. I hate diplomacy. It means fraud and cowardice. Don't you think I know him? The gentleman with the cross of white ribbon on his breast? I know the Marquis d'Harmonville perfectly. You see to what good purpose your ingenuity has been expended."

"To that conjecture I can answer neither yes nor no."

"You need not. But what was your motive in mortifying a lady?"

"It is the last thing on earth I should do."

"You affected to know me, and you don't; through caprice, or listlessness, or curiosity, you wished to converse, not with a lady, but with a costume. You admired, and you pretend to mistake me for another. But who is quite perfect? Is truth any longer to be found on earth?"

"Mademoiselle has formed a mistaken opinion of me."

"And you also of me; you find me less foolish than you supposed. I know perfectly whom you intend amusing with compliments and melancholy declamation, and whom, with that amiable purpose, you have been seeking."

"Tell me whom you mean," I entreated. "Upon one condition."

"What is that?"

"That you will confess if I name the lady."

"You describe my object unfairly," I objected. "I can't admit that I proposed speaking to any lady in the tone you describe."

"Well, I shan't insist on that; only if I name the lady, you will promise to admit that I am right."

"*Must* I promise?"

"Certainly not, there is no compulsion; but your promise is the only condition on which I will speak to you again."

I hesitated for a moment; but how could she possibly tell? The Countess would scarcely have admitted this little romance to anyone; and the mask in the La Vallière costume could not possibly know who the masked domino beside her was.

"I consent," I said, "I promise."

"You must promise on the honor of a gentleman."

"Well, I do; on the honor of a gentleman."

"Then this lady is the Countess de St. Alyre."

I was unspeakably surprised; I was disconcerted; but I remembered my promise, and said:

"The Countess de St. Alyre *is*, unquestionably, the lady to whom I hoped for an introduction tonight; but I beg to assure you, also on the honor of a gentleman, that she has not the faintest imaginable suspicion that I was seeking such an honor, nor, in all probability, does she remember that such a person as I exists. I had the honor to render her and the Count a trifling service, too trifling, I fear, to have earned more than an hour's recollection."

"The world is not so ungrateful as you suppose; or if it be, there are, nevertheless, a few hearts that redeem it. I can answer for the Countess de St. Alyre, she never forgets a kindness. She does not show all she feels; for she is unhappy, and cannot."

"Unhappy! I feared, indeed, that might be. But for all the rest that you are good enough to suppose, it is but a flattering dream."

"I told you that I am the Countess's friend, and being so I must know something of her character; also, there are confidences between us, and I may know more than you think of those trifling services of which you suppose the recollection is so transitory."

I was becoming more and more interested. I was as wicked as other young men, and the heinousness of such a pursuit was as nothing, now that self-love and all the passions that mingle in such a romance were roused. The image of the beautiful Countess had now again quite superseded the pretty counterpart of La Valliée, who was before me. I would have given a great deal to hear, in solemn earnest, that she did remember the champion who, for her sake, had thrown himself before the saber of an enraged dragoon, with only a cudgel in his hand, and conquered.

"You say the Countess is unhappy," said I. "What causes her unhappiness?"

"Many things. Her husband is old, jealous, and tyrannical. Is not that enough? Even when relieved from his society, she is lonely."

"But you are her friend?" I suggested.

"And you think one friend enough?" she answered; "she has one alone, to whom she can open her heart."

"Is there room for another friend?"

"Try."

"How can I find a way?"

"She will aid you."

"How?"

She answered by a question. "Have you secured rooms in either of the hotels of Versailles?"

"No, I could not. I am lodged in the Dragon Volant, which stands at the verge of the grounds of the Château de la Carque."

"That is better still. I need not ask if you have courage for an adventure. I need not ask if you are a man of honor. A lady may trust herself to you, and fear nothing. There are few men to whom the interview, such as I shall arrange, could be granted with safety. You shall meet her at two o'clock this morning in the Park of the Château de la Carque. What room do you occupy in the Dragon Volant?"

I was amazed at the audacity and decision of this girl. Was she, as we say in England, hoaxing me?

"I can describe that accurately," said I. "As I look from the rear of the house, in which my apartment is, I am at the extreme right, next the angle; and one pair of stairs up, from the hall."

"Very well; you must have observed, if you looked into the park, two or three clumps of chestnut and lime trees, growing so close together as to form a small grove. You must return to your hotel, change your dress, and, preserving a scrupulous secrecy as to why or where you go, leave the Dragon Volant, and climb the park wall, unseen; you will easily recognize the grove I have mentioned; there you will meet the Countess, who will grant you an audience of a few minutes, who will expect the most scrupulous reserve on your part, and who will explain to you, in a few words, a great deal which I could not so well tell you here."

I cannot describe the feeling with which I heard these words. I was astounded. Doubt succeeded. I could not believe these agitating words.

"Mademoiselle will believe that if I only dared assure myself that so great a happiness and honor were really intended for me, my gratitude would be as lasting as my life. But how dare I believe that Mademoiselle does not speak, rather from her own sympathy or goodness, than from a certainty that the Countess de St. Alyre would concede so great an honor?"

"Monsieur believes either that I am not, as I pretend to be, in the secret which he hitherto supposed to be shared by no one but the Countess and himself, or else that I am cruelly mystifying him. That I am in her confidence, I swear by all that is dear in a whispered farewell. By the last companion of this flower!" and she took for a moment in her fingers the nodding head of a white rosebud that was nestled in her bouquet. "By my own good star, and hers—or shall I call it our 'belle étoile?' Have I said enough?"

"Enough?" I repeated, "more than enough—a thousand thanks."

"And being thus in her confidence, I am clearly her friend; and being a friend would it be friendly to use her dear name so; and all for sake of practicing a vulgar trick upon you—a stranger?"

"Mademoiselle will forgive me. Remember how very precious is the hope of seeing, and speaking to the Countess. Is it wonderful, then, that I should falter in my belief? You have convinced me, however, and will forgive my hesitation."

"You will be at the place I have described, then, at two o'clock?"

"Assuredly," I answered.

"And Monsieur, I know, will not fail through fear. No, he need not assure me; his courage is already proved."

"No danger, in such a case, will be unwelcome to me."

"Had you not better go now, Monsieur, and rejoin your friend?"

"I promised to wait here for my friend's return. The Count de St. Alyre said that he intended to introduce me to the Countess."

"And Monsieur is so simple as to believe him?"

"Why should I not?"

"Because he is jealous and cunning. You will see. He will never introduce you to his wife. He will come here and say he cannot find her, and promise another time."

"I think I see him approaching, with my friend. No—there is no lady with him."

"I told you so. You will wait a long time for that happiness, if it is never to reach you except through his hands. In the meantime, you had better not let him see you so near me. He will suspect that we have been talking of his wife; and that will whet his jealousy and his vigilance."

I thanked my unknown friend in the mask, and withdrawing a few steps, came, by a little "circumbendibus," upon the flank of the Count. I smiled under my mask as he assured me that the Duchess de la Roqueme had changed her place, and taken the Countess with her; but he hoped, at some very early time, to have an opportunity of enabling her to make my acquaintance.

I avoided the Marquis d'Harmonville, who was following the Count. I was afraid he might propose accompanying me home, and had no wish to be forced to make an explanation.

I lost myself quickly, therefore, in the crowd, and moved, as rapidly as it would allow me, toward the Galerie des Glaces, which lay in the direction opposite to that in which I saw the Count and my friend the Marquis moving.

CHAPTER FIFTEEN

STRANGE STORY OF THE DRAGON VOLANT

These *fêtes* were earlier in those days, and in France, than our modern balls are in London. I consulted my watch. It was a little past twelve.

It was a still and sultry night; the magnificent suite of rooms, vast as some of them were, could not be kept at a temperature less than oppressive, especially to people with masks on. In some places the crowd was inconvenient, and the profusion of lights added to the heat. I removed my mask, therefore, as I saw some other people do, who were as careless of mystery as I. I had hardly done so, and began to breathe more comfortably, when I heard a friendly English voice call me by my name. It was Tom Whistlewick, of the —th Dragoons. He had unmasked, with a very flushed face, as I did. He was one of those Waterloo heroes, new from the mint of glory, whom, as a body, all the world,. except France, revered; and the only thing I knew against him, was a habit of allaying his thirst, which was excessive at balls, *fêtes,* musical parties, and all gatherings, where it was to be had, with champagne; and, as he introduced me to his friend, Monsieur Carmaignac, I observed that he spoke a little thick. Monsieur Carmaignac was little, lean, and as straight as a ramrod. He was bald, took snuff, and wore spectacles; and, as I soon learned, held an official position.

Tom was facetious, sly, and rather difficult to understand, in his present pleasant mood. He was elevating his eyebrows and screwing his lips oddly, and fanning himself vaguely with his mask.

After some agreeable conversation I was glad to observe that he preferred silence, and was satisfied with the *rôle* of listener, as I and Monsieur Carmaignac chatted; and he seated himself, with extraordinary caution and indecision, upon a bench, beside us, and seemed very soon to find a difficulty in keeping his eyes open.

"I heard you mention," said the French gentleman, "that you had engaged an apartment in the Dragon Volant, about half a league from this. When I was in a different police department, about four years ago, two very strange cases were connected with that house. One was of a wealthy *émigré*, permitted to return to France by the Em—by Napoleon. He vanished. The other—equally strange—was the case of a Russian of rank and wealth. He disappeared just as mysteriously."

"My servant," I said, "gave me a confused account of some occurrences, and, as well as I recollect, he described the same persons—I mean a returned French nobleman and a Russian gentleman. But he made the whole story so marvelous—I mean in the supernatural sense—that, I confess, I did not believe a word of it."

"No, there was nothing supernatural; but a great deal inexplicable," said the French gentleman. "Of course, there may be theories; but the thing was never explained, nor, so far as I know, was a ray of light ever thrown upon it."

"Pray let me hear the story," I said. "I think I have a claim, as it affects my quarters. You don't suspect the people of the house?"

"Oh! it has changed hands since then. But there seemed to be a fatality about a particular room."

"Could you describe that room?"

"Certainly. It is a spacious, paneled bedroom, up one pair of stairs, in the back of the house, and at the extreme right, as you look from its windows."

"Ho! Really? Why, then, I have got the very room!" I said, beginning to be more interested—perhaps the least bit in the world, disagreeably. "Did the people die, or were they actually spirited away?"

"No, they did not die—they disappeared very oddly. I'll tell you the particulars—I happen to know them exactly, because I made an official visit, on the first occasion, to the house, to collect evidence; and although I did not go down there, upon the second, the papers came before me, and I dictated the official letter dispatched to the relations of the people who had disappeared; they had applied to the government to investigate the affair. We had letters from the same relations more than two years later, from which we learned that the missing men had never turned up."

He took a pinch of snuff, and looked steadily at me.

"Never! I shall relate all that happened, so far as we could discover. The French noble, who was the Chevalier Chateau Blassemare, unlike most *émigrés* had taken the matter in time, sold a large portion of his property before the revolution had proceeded so far as to render that next to impossible, and retired with a large sum. He brought with him about half a million of francs, the greater part of which he invested in the French funds; a much larger sum remained in Austrian land and securities. You will observe then that this gentleman was rich, and there was no allegation of his having lost money, or being in any way embarrassed. You see?"

I assented.

"This gentleman's habits were not expensive in proportion to his means. He had suitable lodgings in Paris; and for a time, society, and theaters, and other reasonable amusements, engrossed him. He did not play. He was a middleaged man, affecting youth, with the vanities which are usual in such persons; but, for the rest, he was a gentle and polite person, who disturbed nobody—a person, you see, not likely to provoke an enmity."

"Certainly not," I agreed.

"Early in the summer of 1811 he got an order permitting him to copy a picture in one of these *salons,* and came down here, to Versailles, for the purpose. His work was getting on slowly. After a time he left his hotel here, and went, by way of change, to the Dragon Volant; there he took, by special choice, the bedroom which has fallen to you by chance. From this time, it appeared, he painted little; and seldom visited his apartments in Paris. One night he saw the host of the Dragon Volant, and told him that he was going into Paris, to remain for a day or two, on very particular business; that his servant would accompany him, but that he would retain his apartments at the Dragon Volant, and return in a few days. He left some clothes there, but packed a portmanteau, took his dressing case and the rest, and, with his servant behind his carriage, drove into Paris. You observe all this, Monsieur?"

"Most attentively," I answered.

"Well, Monsieur, as soon as they were approaching his lodgings, he stopped the carriage on a sudden, told his servant that he had changed his mind; that he would sleep elsewhere that night, that he had very particular business in the north of France, not far from Rouen, that he would set out before daylight on his journey, and return in a fortnight. He called a *fiacre,* took in his hand a leather bag which, the servant said, was just large enough to hold a few shirts and a coat, but that it was enormously heavy, as he could testify, for he held it in his hand, while his master took out his purse to count thirty-six Napoleons, for which the servant was to account when he should return. He then sent him on, in the carriage; and he, with the bag I have mentioned, got into the *fiacre.* Up to that, you see, the narrative is quite clear."

"Perfectly," I agreed.

"Now comes the mystery," said Monsieur Carmaignac. "After that, the Count Chateau Blassemare was never more seen, so far as we can make out, by acquaintance or friend. We learned that the day before the Count's stockbroker had, by his direction, sold all his stock in the French funds, and handed him the cash it realized. The reason he gave him for this measure tallied with what he said to his servant. He told him that he was going to the north of France to settle some claims, and did not know exactly how much might be required. The bag, which had puzzled the servant by its weight, contained, no doubt, a large sum in gold. Will Monsieur try my snuff?"

He politely tendered his open snuff-box, of which I partook, experimentally.

"A reward was offered," he continued, "when the inquiry was instituted, for any information tending to throw a light upon the mystery, which might be afforded by the driver of the *fiacre* 'employed on the night of'(so-and-so), 'at about the hour of half-past ten, by a gentleman, with a black-leather bag-bag in his hand, who descended from a private carriage, and gave his servant some money, which he counted twice over.' About a hundred-and-fifty drivers applied, but not one of them was the right man. We did, however, elicit a curious and unexpected piece of evidence in quite another quarter. What a racket that plaguey harlequin makes with his sword!"

"Intolerable!" I chimed in.

The harlequin was soon gone, and he resumed.

"The evidence I speak of came from a boy, about twelve years old, who knew the appearance of the Count perfectly, having been often employed by him as a messenger. He stated that about half-past twelve o'clock, on the same night—upon which you are to observe, there was a brilliant moon—he was sent, his mother having been suddenly taken ill, for the sage *femme* who lived within a stone's throw of the Dragon Volant. His father's house, from which he started, was a mile away, or more, from that inn, in order to reach which he had to pass round the park of the Chéteau de la Carque, at the site most remote from the point to which he was going. It passes the old churchyard of St. Aubin, which is separated from the road only by a very low fence, and two or three enormous old trees. The boy was a little nervous as he approached this ancient cemetery; and, under the bright moonlight, he saw a man whom he distinctly recognized as the Count, whom they designated by a sobriquet which means 'the man of smiles.' He was looking rueful enough now, and was seated on the side of a tombstone, on which he had laid a pistol, while he was ramming home the charge of another.

"The boy got cautiously by, on tiptoe, with his eyes all the time on the Count Chateau Blassernare, or the man he mistook for him—his dress was not what he usually wore, but the witness swore that he could not be mistaken as to his identity. He said his face looked grave and stern; but though he did not smile, it was the same face he knew so well. Nothing would make him swerve from that. If that were he, it was the last time he was seen. He has never been heard of since. Nothing could be heard of him in the neighborhood of Rouen. There has been no evidence of his death; and there is no sign that he is living."

"That certainly is a most singular case," I replied, and was about to ask a question or two, when Tom Whistlewick who, without my observing it, had been taking a ramble, returned, a great deal more awake, and a great deal less tipsy.

"I say, Carmaignac, it is getting late, and I must go; I really must, for the reason I told you—and, Beckett, we must soon meet again."

"I regret very much, Monsieur, my not being able at present to relate to you the other case, that of another tenant of the very same room—a case more mysterious and sinister than the last—and which occurred in the autumn of the same year."

"Will you both do a very good-natured thing, and come and dine with me at the Dragon Volant tomorrow?"

So, as we pursued our way along the Galerie des Glaces, I extracted their promise.

"By Jove!" said Whistlewick, when this was done; "look at that pagoda, or sedan chair, or whatever it is, just where those fellows set it down, and not one of them near it! I can't imagine how they tell fortunes so devilish well. Jack Nuffles—I met him here tonight—says they are gypsies—where are they, I wonder? I'll go over and have a peep at the prophet."

I saw him plucking at the blinds, which were constructed something on the principle of Venetian blinds; the red curtains were inside; but they did not yield, and he could only peep under one that did not come quite down.

When he rejoined us, he related: "I could scarcely see the old fellow, it's so dark. He is covered with gold and red, and has an embroidered hat on like a mandarin's; he's fast asleep; and, by Jove, he smells like a polecat! It's worth going over only to have it to say. Fiew! pooh! oh! It is a perfume. Faugh!"

Not caring to accept this tempting invitation, we got along slowly toward the door. I bade them good-night, reminding them of their promise. And so found my way at last to my carriage; and was soon rolling slowly toward the Dragon Volant, on the loneliest of roads, under old trees, and the soft moonlight.

What a number of things had happened within the last two hours! What a variety of strange and vivid pictures were crowded together in that brief space! What an adventure was before me!

The silent, moonlighted, solitary road, how it contrasted with the many-eddied whirl of pleasure from whose roar and music, lights, diamonds and colors I had just extricated myself.

The sight of lonely nature at such an hour, acts like a sudden sedative. The madness and guilt of my pursuit struck me with a momentary compunction and horror. I wished I had never entered the labyrinth which was leading me, I knew not whither. It was too late to think of that now; but the bitter was already stealing into my cup; and vague anticipations lay, for a few minutes, heavy on my heart. It would not have taken much to make me disclose my unmanly state of mind to my lively friend Alfred Ogle, nor even to the milder ridicule of the agreeable Tom Whistlewick.

CHAPTER SIXTEEN

THE PARC OF THE CHÂTEAU DE LA CARQUE

There was no danger of the Dragon Volant's closing its doors on that occasion till three or four in the morning. There were quartered there many servants of great people, whose masters would not leave the ball till the last moment, and who could not return to their corners in the Dragon Volant till their last services had been rendered.

I knew, therefore, I should have ample time for my mysterious excursion without exciting curiosity by being shut out.

And now we pulled up under the canopy of boughs, before the sign of the Dragon Volant, and the light that shone from its hall-door.

I dismissed my carriage, ran up the broad stair-case, mask in hand, with my domino fluttering about me, and entered the large bedroom. The black wainscoting and stately furniture, with the dark curtains of the very tall bed, made the night there more somber.

An oblique patch of moonlight was thrown upon the floor from the window to which I hastened. I looked out upon the landscape slumbering in those silvery beams. There stood the outline of the Château de la Carque, its chimneys and many turrets with their extinguisher-shaped roofs black against the soft grey sky. There, also, more in the foreground, about midway between the window where I stood and the château, but a little to the left, I traced the tufted masses of the grove which the lady in the mask had appointed as the trysting-place, where I and the beautiful Countess were to meet that night.

I took "the bearings" of this gloomy bit of wood, whose foliage glimmered softly at top in the light of the moon.

You may guess with what a strange interest and swelling of the heart I gazed on the unknown scene of my coming adventure.

But time was flying, and the hour already near. I threw my robe upon a sofa; I groped out a pair of hoots, which I substituted for those thin heelless shoes, in those days called "pumps," without which a gentleman could not attend an evening party. I put on my hat and, lastly, I took a pair of loaded pistols, which I had been advised were satisfactory companions in the then unsettled state of French society; swarms of disbanded soldiers, some of them alleged to be desperate characters, being everywhere to be met with. These preparations made, I confess I took a looking-glass to the window to see how I looked in the moonlight; and being satisfied, I replaced it, and ran downstairs.

In the hall I called for my servant.

"St. Clair," said I; "I mean to take a little moonlight ramble, only ten minutes or so. You must not go to bed until I return. If the night is very beautiful, I may possibly extend my ramble a little."

So down the steps I lounged, looking first over my right, and then over my left shoulder, like a man uncertain which direction to take, and I sauntered up the road, gazing now at the moon, and now at the thin white clouds in the opposite direction, whistling, all the time, an air which I had picked up at one of the theatres.

When I had got a couple of hundred yards away from the Dragon Volant, my minstrelsy totally ceased; and I turned about, and glanced sharply down the road, that looked as white as hoar-frost under the moon, and saw the gable of the old inn, and a window, partly concealed by the foliage, with a dusky light shining from it.

No sound of footstep was stirring; no sign of human figure in sight. I consulted my watch, which the light was sufficiently strong to enable me to do. It now wanted but eight minutes of the appointed hour. A thick mantle of ivy at this point covered the wall and rose in a clustering head at top.

It afforded me facilities for scaling the wall, and a partial screen for my operations if any eye should chance to be looking that way. And now it was done. I was in the park of the Château de la Carque, as nefarious a poacher as ever trespassed on the grounds of unsuspicious lord!

Before me rose the appointed grove, which looked as black as a clump of gigantic hearse plumes. It seemed to tower higher and higher at every step; and cast a broader and blacker shadow toward my feet. On I marched, and was glad when I plunged into the shadow which concealed me. Now I was among the grand old lime and chestnut trees—my heart beat fast with expectation.

This grove opened, a little, near the middle; and, in the space thus cleared, there stood with a surrounding flight of steps a small Greek temple or shrine, with a statue in the center. It was built of white marble with fluted Corinthian columns, and the crevices were tufted with grass; moss had shown itself on pedestal and cornice, and signs of long neglect and decay were apparent in its discolored and weather-worn marble. A few feet in front of the steps a fountain, fed from the great ponds at the other side of the château, was making a constant tinkle and splashing in a wide marble basin, and the jet of water glimmered like a shower of diamonds in the broken moonlight. The very neglect and half-ruinous state of all this made it only the prettier, as well as sadder. I was too intently watching for the arrival of the lady, in the direction of the château, to study these things; but the half-noted effect of them was romantic, and suggested somehow the grotto and the fountain, and the apparition of Egeria.

As I watched a voice spoke to me, a little behind my left shoulder. I turned, almost with a start, and the masque, in the costume of Mademoiselle de la Vallière, stood there.

"The Countess will be here presently," she said. The lady stood upon the open space, and the moonlight fell unbroken upon her. Nothing could be more becoming; her figure looked more graceful and elegant than ever. "In the meantime I shall tell you some peculiarities of her situation. She is unhappy; miserable in an ill—assorted marriage, with a jealous tyrant who now would constrain her to sell her diamonds, which are—"

"Worth thirty thousand pounds sterling. I heard all that from a friend. Can I aid the Countess in her unequal struggle? Say but how the greater the danger or the sacrifice, the happier will it make me. *Can* I aid her?"

"If you despise a danger—which, yet, is not a danger; if you despise, as she does, the tyrannical canons of the world; and if you are chivalrous enough to devote yourself to a lady's cause, with no reward but her poor gratitude; if you can do these things you can aid her, and earn a foremost place, not in her gratitude only, but in her friendship."

At those words the lady in the mask turned away and seemed to weep.

I vowed myself the willing slave of the Countess. "But," I added, "you told me she would soon be here."

"That is, if nothing unforeseen should happen; but with the eye of the Count de St. Alyre in the house, and open, it is seldom safe to stir."

"Does she wish to see me?" I asked, with a tender hesitation.

"First, say have you really thought of her, more than once, since the adventure of the Belle Étoile?"

"She never leaves my thoughts; day and night her beautiful eyes haunt me; her sweet voice is always in my ear."

"Mine is said to resemble hers," said the mask.

"So it does," I answered. "But it is only a resemblance."

"Oh! then mine is better?"

"Pardon me, Mademoiselle, I did not say that. Yours is a sweet voice, but I fancy a little higher."

"A little shriller, you would say," answered the De la Vallière, I fancied a good deal vexed.

"No, not shriller: your voice is not shrill, it is beautifully sweet; but not so pathetically sweet as hers."

"That is prejudice, Monsieur; it is not true."

I bowed; I could not contradict a lady.

"I see, Monsieur, you laugh at me; you think me vain, because I claim in some points to be equal to the Countess de St. Alyre. I challenge you to say, my hand, at least, is less beautiful than hers." As she thus spoke she drew her glove off, and extended her hand, back upward, in the moonlight.

The lady seemed really nettled. It was undignified and irritating; for in this uninteresting competition the precious moments were flying, and my interview leading apparently to nothing.

"You will admit, then, that my hand is as beautiful as hers?"

"I cannot admit it. Mademoiselle," said I, with the honesty of irritation. "I will not enter into comparisons, but the Countess de St. Alyre is, in all respects, the most beautiful lady I ever beheld."

The masque laughed coldly, and then, more and more softly, said, with a sigh, "I will prove all I say." And as she spoke she removed the mask: and the Countess de St. Alyre, smiling, confused, bashful, more beautiful than ever, stood before me!

"Good Heavens!" I exclaimed. "How monstrously stupid I have been. And it was to Madame la Comtesse that I spoke for so long in the *salon*!" I gazed on her in silence. And with a low sweet laugh of good nature she extended her hand. I took it and carried it to my lips.

"No, you must not do that," she said quietly, "we are not old enough friends yet. I find, although you were mistaken, that you do remember the Countess of the Belle Étoile, and that you are a champion true and fearless. Had you yielded to the claims just now pressed upon you by the rivalry of Mademoiselle de la Valière, in her mask, the Countess de St. Alyre should never have trusted or seen you more. I now am sure that you are true, as well as brave. You now know that I have not forgotten you; and, also, that if you would risk your life for me, I, too, would brave some danger, rather than lose my friend forever. I have but a few moments more. Will you come here again tomorrow night, at a quarter past eleven? I will be here at that moment; you must exercise the most scrupulous care to prevent suspicion that you have come here, Monsieur. *You owe that to me.*"

She spoke these last words with the most solemn entreaty.

I vowed again and again that I would die rather than permit the least rashness to endanger the secret which made all the interest and value of my life.

She was looking, I thought, more and more beautiful every moment. My enthusiasm expanded in proportion.

"You must come tomorrow night by a different route," she said; "and if you come again, we can change it once more. At the other side of the château there is a little churchyard, with a ruined chapel. The neighbors are afraid to pass it by night. The road is deserted there, and a stile opens a way into these grounds. Cross it and you can find a covert of thickets, to within fifty steps of this spot."

I promised, of course, to observe her instructions implicitly.

"I have lived for more than a year in an agony of irresolution. I have decided at last. I have lived a melancholy life; a lonelier life than is passed in the cloister. I have had no one to confide in; no one to advise me; no one to save me from the horrors of my existence. I have found a brave and prompt friend at last. Shall I ever forget the heroic tableau of the hall of the Belle Étoile? Have you—have you really kept the rose I gave you, as we parted? Yes—you swear it. You need not; I trust you. Richard, how often have I in solitude repeated your name, learned from my servant. Richard, my hero! Oh! Richard! Oh, my king! I love you!"

I would have folded her to my heart—thrown myself at her feet. But this beautiful and—shall I say it—inconsistent woman repelled me.

"No, we must not waste our moments in extravagances. Understand my case. There is no such thing as indifference in the married state. Not to love one's husband," she continued, "is to hate him. The Count, ridiculous in all else, is formidable in his jealousy. In mercy, then, to me, observe caution. Affect to all you speak to, the most complete ignorance of all the people in the Château de la Carque; and, if anyone in your presence mentions the Count or Countess de St. Alyre, be sure you say you never saw either. I shall have more to say to you tomorrow night. I have reasons that I cannot now explain, for all I do, and all I postpone. Farewell. Go! Leave me."

She waved me back, peremptorily. I echoed her "farewell," and obeyed.

This interview had not lasted, I think, more than ten minutes. I scaled the park wall again, and reached the Dragon Volant before its doors were closed.

I lay awake in my bed, in a fever of elation. I saw, till the dawn broke, and chased the vision, the beautiful Countess de St. Alyre, always in the dark, before me.

CHAPTER SEVENTEEN

THE TENANT OF THE PALANQUIN

The Marquis called on me next day. My late breakfast was still upon the table. He had come, he said, to ask a favor. An accident had happened to his carriage in the crowd on leaving the ball, and he begged, if I were going into Paris, a seat in mine. I was going in, and was extremely glad of his company. He came with me to my hotel; we went up to my rooms. I was surprised to see a man seated in an easy chair, with his back towards us, reading a newspaper. He rose. It was the Count de St. Alyre, his gold spectacles on his nose; his black wig, in oily curls, lying close to his narrow head, and showing like carved ebony over a repulsive visage of boxwood. His black muffler had been pulled down. His. right arm was in a sling. I don't know whether there was anything unusual in his countenance that day, or whether it was but the effect of prejudice arising from all I had heard in my mysterious interview in his park, but I thought his countenance was more strikingly forbidding than I had seen it before.

I was not callous enough in the ways of sin to meet this man, injured at least in intent, thus suddenly, without a momentary disturbance.

He smiled.

"I called, Monsieur Beckett, in the hope of finding you here," he croaked, "and I meditated, I fear, taking a great liberty, but my friend the

Marquis d'Harmonville, on whom I have perhaps some claim, will perhaps give me the assistance I require so much."

"With great pleasure," said the Marquis, "but not till after six o'clock. I must go this moment to a meeting of three or four people whom I cannot disappoint, and I know, perfectly, we cannot break up earlier."

"What am I to do?" exclaimed the Count, "an hour would have done it all. Was ever *contretemps* so unlucky?"

"I'll give you an hour, with pleasure," said I.

"How very good of you, Monsieur, I hardly dare to hope it. The business, for so gay and charming a man as Monsieur Beckett, is a little *funeste*. Pray read this note which reached me this morning."

It certainly was not cheerful. It was a note stating that the body of his, the Count's cousin, Monsieur de St. Amand, who had died at his house, the Château Clery, had been, in accordance with his written directions, sent for burial at Père la Chaise, and, with the permission of the Count de St. Alyre, would reach his house (the Château de la Carque) at about ten o'clock on the night following, to be conveyed thence in a hearse, with any member of the family who might wish to attend the obsequies.

"I did not see the poor gentleman twice in my life," said the Count, "but this office, as he has no other kinsman, disagreeable as it is, I could scarcely decline, and so I want to attend at the office to have the book signed, and the order entered. But here is another misery. By ill luck I have sprained my thumb, and can't sign my name for a week to come. However, one name answers as well as another. Yours as well as mine. And as you are so good as to come with me, all will go right."

Away we drove. The Count gave me a memorandum of the Christian and surnames of the deceased, his age, the complaint he died of, and the usual particulars; also a note of the exact position in which a grave, the dimensions of which were described, of the ordinary simple kind, was to be dug, between two vaults belonging to the family of St. Amand. The funeral, it was stated, would arrive at half—past one o'clock A.M.

(the next night but one); and he handed me the money, with extra fees, for a burial by night. It was a good deal; and I asked him, as he entrusted the whole affair to me, in whose name I should take the receipt.

"Not in mine, my good friend. They wanted me to become an executor, which I, yesterday, wrote to decline; and I am informed that if the receipt were in my name it would constitute me an executor in the eye of the law, and fix me in that position. Take it, pray, if you have no objection, in your own name."

This, accordingly, I did.

You will see, by—and—by, why I am obliged to mention all these particulars.

The Count, meanwhile, was leaning back in the carriage, with his black silk muffler up to his nose, and his hat shading his eyes, while he dozed in his corner; in which state I found him on my return.

Paris had lost its charm for me. I hurried through the little business I had to do, longed once more for my quiet room in the Dragon Volant, the melancholy woods of the Château de la Carque, and the tumultuous and thrilling influence of proximity to the object of my wild but wicked romance.

I was delayed some time by my stockbroker. I had a very large sum, as I told you, at my banker's, uninvested. I cared very little for a few day's interest—very little for the entire sum, compared with the image that occupied my thoughts, and beckoned me with a white arm, through the dark, toward the spreading lime trees and chestnuts of the Château de la Carque. But I had fixed this day to meet him, and was relieved when he told me that I had better let it lie in my banker's hands for a few days longer, as the funds would certainly fall immediately. This accident, too, was not without its immediate bearing on my subsequent adventures.

When I reached the Dragon Volant, I found, in my sitting-room, a good deal to my chagrin, my two guests, whom I had quite forgotten. I inwardly cursed my own stupidity for having embarrassed myself with their agreeable society. It could not be helped now, however, and a word to the waiters put all things in train for dinner.

Tom Whistlewick was in great force; and he commenced almost immediately with a very odd story.

He told me that not only Versailles, but all Paris was in a ferment, in consequence of a revolting, and all but sacrilegious practical joke, played of on the night before.

The pagoda, as he persisted in calling the palanquin, had been left standing on the spot where we last saw it. Neither conjuror, nor usher, nor bearers had ever returned. When the ball closed, and the company at length retired, the servants who attended to put out the lights, and secure the doors, found it still there.

It was determined, however, to let it stand where it was until next morning, by which time, it was conjectured, its owners would send messengers to remove it.

None arrived. The servants were then ordered to take it away; and its extraordinary weight, for the first time, reminded them of its forgotten human occupant. Its door was forced; and, judge what was their disgust, when they discovered, not a living man, but a corpse! Three or four days must have passed since the death of the burly man in the Chinese tunic and painted cap. Some people thought it was a trick designed to insult the Allies, in whose honor the ball was got up. Others were of opinion that it was nothing worse than a daring and cynical jocularity which, shocking as it was, might yet be forgiven to the high spirits and irrepressible buffoonery of youth. Others, again, fewer in number, and mystically given, insisted that the corpse was *bona fide* necessary to the exhibition, and that the disclosures and allusions which had astonished so many people were distinctly due to necromancy.

"The matter, however, is now in the hands of the police," observed Monsieur Carmaignac, "and we are not the body they were two or three months ago, if the offenders against propriety and public feeling are not traced and convicted, unless, indeed, they have been a great deal more cunning than such fools generally are."

I was thinking within myself how utterly inexplicable was my colloquy with the conjuror, so cavalierly dismissed by Monsieur Carmaignac as a "fool"; and the more I thought the more marvelous it seemed.

"It certainly was an original joke, though not a very clear one," said Whistlewick.

"Not even original," said Carmaignac. "Very nearly the same thing was done, a hundred years ago or more, at a state ball in Paris; and the rascals who played the trick were never found out."

In this Monsieur Carmaignac, as I afterwards discovered, spoke truly; for, among my books of French anecdote and memoirs, the very incident is marked by my own hand.

While we were thus talking the waiter told us that dinner was served, and we withdrew accordingly; my guests more than making amends for my comparative taciturnity.

CHAPTER EIGHTEEN

THE CHURCHYARD

Our dinner was really good, so were the wines; better, perhaps, at this out-of-the-way inn, than at some of the more pretentious hotels in Paris. The moral effect of a really good dinner is immense—we all felt it. The serenity and good nature that follow are more solid and comfortable than the tumultuous benevolences of Bacchus.

My friends were happy, therefore, and very chatty; which latter relieved me of the trouble of talking, and prompted them to entertain me and one another incessantly with agreeable stories and conversation, of which, until suddenly a subject emerged which interested me powerfully, I confess, so much were my thoughts engaged elsewhere, I heard next to nothing.

"Yes," said Carmaignac, continuing a conversation which had escaped me, "there was another case, beside that Russian nobleman, odder still. I remembered it this morning, but cannot recall the name. He was a tenant of the very same room. By-the-by, Monsieur, might it not be as well," he added, turning to me with a laugh, half joke whole earnest, as they say, "if you were to get into another apartment, now that the house is no longer crowded? that is, if you mean to make any stay here."

"A thousand thanks! no. I'm thinking of changing my hotel; and I can run into town so easily at night; and though I stay here for this night at least, I don't expect to vanish like those others. But you say there is another adventure, of the same kind, connected with the same room. Do let us hear it. But take some wine first."

The story he told was curious.

"It happened," said Carmaignac, "as well as I recollect, before either of the other cases. A French gentleman—I wish I could remember his name—the son of a merchant, came to this inn (the Dragon Volant), and was put by the landlord into the same room of which we have been speaking. Your apartment, Monsieur. He was by no means young—past forty—and very far from good-looking. The people here said that he was the ugliest man, and the most good-natured, that ever lived. He played on the fiddle, sang, and wrote poetry. His habits were odd and desultory. He would sometimes sit all day in his room writing, singing, and fiddling, and go out at night for a walk. An eccentric man! He was by no means a millionaire, but he had a *modicum bonum,* you understand—a trifle more than half a million of francs. He consulted his stockbroker about investing this money in foreign stocks, and drew the entire sum from his banker. You now have the situation of affairs when the catastrophe occurred."

"Pray fill your glass," I said.

"Dutch courage, Monsieur, to face the catastrophe!" said Whistlewick, filling his own.

"Now, that was the last that ever was heard of his money," resumed Carmaignac. "You shall hear about himself. The night after this financial operation he was seized with a poetic frenzy: he sent for the then landlord of this house, and told him that he long meditated an epic, and meant to commence that night, and that he was on no account to be disturbed until nine o'clock in the morning. He had two pairs of wax candles, a little cold supper on a side-table, his desk open, paper enough upon it to contain the entire *Henriade,* and a proportionate store of pens and ink.

"Seated at this desk he was seen by the waiter who brought him a cup of coffee at nine o'clock, at which time the intruder said he was writing fast enough to set fire to the paper—that was his phrase; he did not look up, he appeared too much engrossed. But when the waiter came back, half an hour afterwards, the door was locked; and the poet, from within, answered that he must not be disturbed.

"Away went the *garçon,* and next morning at nine o'clock knocked at his door and, receiving no answer, looked through the key-hole; the lights were still burning, the window-shutters were closed as he had left them; he renewed his knocking, knocked louder, no answer came. He reported this continued and alarming silence to the innkeeper, who, finding that his guest had not left his key in the lock, succeeded in finding another that opened it. The candles were just giving up the ghost in their sockets, but there was light enough to ascertain that the tenant of the room was gone! The bed had not been disturbed; the window-shutter was barred. He must have let himself out, and, locking the door on the outside, put the key in his pocket, and so made his way out of the house. Here, however, was another difficulty: the Dragon Volant shut its doors and made all fast at twelve o'clock; after that hour no one could leave the house, except by obtaining the key and letting himself out, and of necessity leaving the door unsecured, or else by collusion and aid of some person in the house.

"Now it happened that, some time after the doors were secured, at half-past twelve, a servant who had not been apprised of his order to be left undisturbed, seeing a light shine through the key-hole, knocked at the door to inquire whether the poet wanted anything. He was very little obliged to his disturber, and dismissed him with a renewed charge that he was not to be interrupted again during the night. This incident established the fact that he was in the house after the doors had been locked and barred. The inn-keeper himself kept the keys, and swore that he found them hung on the wall above his head, in his bed, in their usual place, in the morning; and that nobody could have taken them away without awakening him. That was all we could discover. The Count de

St. Alyre, to whom this house belongs, was very active and very much chagrined. But nothing was discovered."

"And nothing heard since of the epic poet?" I asked.

"Nothing—not the slightest clue—he never turned up again. I suppose he is dead; if he is not, he must have got into some devilish bad scrape, of which we have heard nothing, that compelled him to abscond with all the secrecy and expedition in his power. All that we know for certain is that, having occupied the room in which you sleep, he vanished, nobody ever knew how, and never was heard of since."

"You have now mentioned three cases," I said, "and all from the same room."

"Three. Yes, all equally unintelligible. When men are murdered, the great and immediate difficulty the assassins encounter is how to conceal the body. It is very hard to believe that three persons should have been consecutively murdered in the same room, and their bodies so effectually disposed of that no trace of them was ever discovered."

From this we passed to other topics, and the grave Monsieur Carmaignac amused us with a perfectly prodigious collection of scandalous anecdote, which his opportunities in the police department had enabled him to accumulate.

My guests happily had engagements in Paris, and left me about ten.

I went up to my room, and looked out upon the grounds of the Château de la Carque. The moonlight was broken by clouds, and the view of the park in this desultory light acquired a melancholy and fantastic character.

The strange anecdotes recounted of the room in which I stood by Monsieur Carmaignac returned vaguely upon my mind, drowning in sudden shadows the gaiety of the more frivolous stories with which he had followed them. I looked round me on the room that lay in ominous gloom, with an almost disagreeable sensation. I took my pistols now with an undefined apprehension that they might be really needed before my return tonight. This feeling, be it understood, in no wise chilled my ardor. Never had my enthusiasm mounted higher. My adventure absorbed and carried me away; but it added a strange and stern excitement to the expedition.

I loitered for a time in my room. I had ascertained the exact point at which the little churchyard lay. It was about a mile away. I did not wish to reach it earlier than necessary.

I stole quietly out and sauntered along the road to my left, and thence entered a narrower track, still to my left, which, skirting the park wall and describing a circuitous route all the way, under grand old trees, passes the ancient cemetery. That cemetery is embowered in trees and occupies little more than half an acre of ground to the left of the road, interposing between it and the park of the Château de la Carque.

Here, at this haunted spot, I paused and listened. The place was utterly silent. A thick cloud had darkened the moon, so that I could distinguish little more than the outlines of near objects, and that vaguely enough; and sometimes, as it were, floating in black fog, the white surface of a tombstone emerged.

Among the forms that met my eye against the iron-grey of the horizon, were some of those shrubs or trees that grow like our junipers, some six feet high, in form like a miniature poplar, with the darker foliage of the yew. I do not know the name of the plant, but I have often seen it in such funereal places.

Knowing that I was a little too early, I sat down upon the edge of a tombstone to wait, as, for aught I knew, the beautiful Countess might have wise reasons for not caring that I should enter the grounds of the château earlier than she had appointed. In the listless state induced by waiting, I sat there, with my eyes on the object straight before me, which chanced to be that faint black outline I have described. It was right before me, about half-a-dozen steps away.

The moon now began to escape from under the skirt of the cloud that had hid her face for so long; and, as the light gradually improved, the tree on which I had been lazily staring began to take a new shape. It was no longer a tree, but a man standing motionless. Brighter and brighter grew the moonlight, clearer and clearer the image became, and at last stood out perfectly distinctly. It was Colonel Gaillarde. Luckily, he was not looking toward me. I could only see him in profile; but there was no mistaking the white moustache, the *farouche* visage, and the gaunt six-foot stature. There he was, his shoulder toward me, listening and watching, plainly, for some signal or person expected, straight in front of him.

If he were, by chance, to turn his eyes in my direction, I knew that I must reckon upon an instantaneous renewal of the combat only commenced in the hall of Belle Étoile. In any case, could malignant fortune have posted, at this place and hour, a more dangerous watcher? What ecstasy to him, by a single discovery, to hit me so hard, and blast the Countess de St. Alyre, whom he seemed to hate.

He raised his arm; he whistled softly; I heard an answering whistle as low; and, to my relief, the Colonel advanced in the direction of this sound, widening the distance between us at every step; and immediately I heard talking, but in a low and cautious key. I recognized, I thought, even so, the peculiar voice of Gaillarde. I stole softly forward in the direction in which those sounds were audible. In doing so, I had, of course, to use the extremest caution.

I thought I saw a hat above a jagged piece of ruined wall, and then a second—yes, I saw two hats conversing; the voices came from under them. They moved off, not in the direction of the park, but of the road, and I lay along the grass, peeping over a grave, as a skirmisher might observing the enemy. One after the other, the figures emerged full into view as they mounted the stile at the roadside. The Colonel, who was last, stood on the wall for awhile, looking about him, and then jumped down on the road. I heard their steps and talk as they moved away together, with their backs toward me, in the direction which led them farther and farther from the Dragon Volant.

I waited until these sounds were quite lost in distance before I entered the park. I followed the instructions I had received from the Countess de St. Alyre, and made my way among brushwood and thickets to the point nearest the ruinous temple, and crossed the short intervening space of open ground rapidly.

I was now once more under the gigantic boughs of the old lime and chestnut trees; softly, and with a heart throbbing fast, I approached the little structure.

The moon was now shining steadily, pouring down its radiance on the soft foliage, and here and there mottling the verdure under my feet.

I reached the steps; I was among its worn marble shafts. She was not there, nor in the inner sanctuary, the arched windows of which were screened almost entirely by masses of ivy. The lady had not yet arrived.

CHAPTER NINETEEN

THE KEY

I stood now upon the steps, watching and listening. In a minute or two I heard the crackle of withered sticks trod upon, and, looking in the direction, I saw a figure approaching among the trees, wrapped in a mantle.

I advanced eagerly. It was the Countess. She did not speak, but gave me her hand, and I led her to the scene of our last interview. She repressed the ardor of my impassioned greeting with a gentle but peremptory firmness. She removed her hood, shook back her beautiful hair, and, gazing on me with sad and glowing eyes, sighed deeply. Some awful thought seemed to weigh upon her,

"Richard, I must speak plainly. The crisis of my life has come. I am sure you would defend me. I think you pity me; perhaps you even love me."

At these words I became eloquent, as young madmen in my plight do. She silenced me, however, with the same melancholy firmness.

"Listen, dear friend, and then say whether you can aid me. How madly I am trusting you; and yet my heart tells me how wisely! To meet you here as I do—what insanity it seems! How poorly you must think of me! But when you know all, you will judge me fairly. Without your aid I cannot accomplish my purpose. That purpose unaccomplished, I must die. I am chained to a man whom I despise—whom I abhor. I have resolved to fly. I have jewels, principally diamonds, for which I am offered thirty thousand pounds of your English money. They are my separate property by my marriage settlement; I will take them with me. You are a judge, no doubt, of jewels. I was counting mine when the hour came, and brought this in my hand to show you. Look."

"It is magnificent!" I exclaimed, as a collar of diamonds twinkled and flashed in the moonlight, suspended from her pretty fingers. I thought, even at that tragic moment, that she prolonged the show, with a feminine delight in these brilliant toys.

"Yes," she said, "I shall part with them all. I will turn them into money and break, forever, the unnatural and wicked bonds that tied me, in the name of a sacrament, to a tyrant. A man young, handsome, generous, brave, as you, can hardly be rich. Richard, you say you love me; you shall share all this with me. We will fly together to Switzerland; we will evade pursuit; in powerful friends will intervene and arrange a separation, and shall, at length, be happy and reward my hero."

You may suppose the style, florid and vehement, in which poured forth my gratitude, vowed the devotion of my life, and placed myself absolutely at her disposal.

"Tomorrow night," she said, "my husband will attend the remains of his cousin, Monsieur de St. Amand, to Père la Chaise. The hearse, he says, will leave this at half-past nine. You must be here, where we stand, at nine o'clock."

I promised punctual obedience.

"I will not meet you here; but you see a red light in the window of the tower at that angle of the château?"

I assented.

"I placed it there, that, tomorrow night, when it comes, you may recognize it. So soon as that rose-colored light appears at that window, it will be a signal to you that the funeral has left the château, and that you may approach safely. Come, then, to that window; I will open it and admit you. Five minutes after a carriage, with four horses, shall stand ready in the *porte-cochère.* I will place my diamonds in your hands; and so soon as we enter the carriage our flight commences. We shall have at least five hours' start; and with energy, stratagem, and resource, I fear nothing. Are you ready to undertake all this for my sake?"

Again I vowed myself her slave.

"My only difficulty," she said, "is how we shall quickly enough convert my diamonds into money; I dare not remove them while my husband is in the house."

Here was the opportunity I wished for. I now told her that I had in my banker's hands no less a sum than thirty thousand pounds, with which, in the shape of gold and notes, I should come furnished, and thus the risk and loss of disposing of her diamonds in too much haste would be avoided.

"Good Heaven!" she exclaimed, with a kind of disappointment. "You are rich, then? and I have lost the felicity of making my generous friend more happy. Be it so! since so it must be. Let us contribute, each, in equal shares, to our common fund. Bring you, your money; I, my jewels. There is a happiness to me even in mingling my resources with yours."

On this there followed a romantic colloquy, all poetry and passion, such as I should in vain endeavor to reproduce. Then came a very special instruction.

"I have come provided, too, with a key, the use of which I must explain."

It was a double key—a long, slender stem, with a key at each end—one about the size which opens an ordinary room door; the other as small, almost, as the key of a dressing-case.

"You cannot employ too much caution tomorrow night. An interruption would murder all my hopes. I have learned that you occupy the haunted room in the Dragon Volant. It is the very room I would have wished you in. I will tell you why—there is a story of a man who, having shut himself up in that room one night, disappeared before morning.

The truth is, he wanted, I believe, to escape from creditors; and the host of the Dragon Volant at that time, being a rogue, aided him in absconding. My husband investigated the matter, and discovered how his escape was made. It was by means of this key. Here is a memorandum and a plan describing how they are to be applied. I have taken them from the Count's escritoire. And now, once more I must leave to your ingenuity how to mystify the people at the Dragon Volant. Be sure you try the keys first, to see that the locks turn freely. I will have my jewels ready. You, whatever we divide, had better bring your money, because it may be many months before you can revisit Paris, or disclose our place of residence to anyone: and our passports—arrange all that; in what names, and whither, you please. And now, dear Richard" (she leaned her arm fondly on my shoulder, and looked with ineffable passion in my eyes, with her other hand clasped in mine), "my very life is in your hands; I have staked all on your fidelity."

As she spoke the last word, she, on a sudden, grew deadly pale, and gasped, "Good God! who is here?"

At the same moment she receded through the door in the marble screen, close to which she stood, and behind which was a small roofless chamber, as small as the shrine, the window of which was darkened by a clustering mass of ivy so dense that hardly a gleam of light came through the leaves.

I stood upon the threshold which she had just crossed, looking in the direction in which she had thrown that one terrified glance. No wonder she was frightened. Quite close upon us, not twenty yards away, and approaching at a quick step, very distinctly lighted by the moon, Colonel Gaillarde and his companion were coming. The shadow of the cornice and a piece of wall were upon me. Unconscious of this, I was expecting the moment when, with one of his frantic yells, he should spring forward to assail me.

I made a step backward, drew one of my pistols from my pocket, and cocked it. It was obvious he had not seen me.

I stood, with my finger on the trigger, determined to shoot him dead if he should attempt to enter the place where the Countess was. It would, no doubt, have been a murder; but, in my mind, I had no question or qualm about it. When once we engage in secret and guilty practices we are nearer other and greater crimes than we at all suspect.

"There's the statue," said the Colonel, in his brief discordant tones. "That's the figure."

"Alluded to in the stanzas?" inquired his companion.

"The very thing. We shall see more next time. Forward, Monsieur; let us march." And, much to my relief, the gallant Colonel turned on his heel and marched through the trees, with his back toward the château, striding over the grass, as I quickly saw, to the park wall, which they crossed not far from the gables of the Dragon Volant.

I found the Countess trembling in no affected, but a very real terror. She would not hear of my accompanying her toward the château. But I told her that I would prevent the return of the mad Colonel; and upon that point, at least, that she need fear nothing. She quickly recovered, again bade me a fond and lingering good-night, and left me, gazing after her, with the key in my hand, and such a phantasmagoria floating in my brain as amounted very nearly to madness.

There was I, ready to brave all dangers, all right and reason, plunge into murder itself, on the first summons, and entangle myself in consequences inextricable and horrible (what cared I?) for a woman of whom I knew nothing, but that she was beautiful and reckless!

I have often thanked heaven for its mercy in conducting me through the labyrinths in which I had all but lost myself.

CHAPTER TWENTY

A HIGH-CAULD-CAP

I was now upon the road, within two or three hundred yards of the Dragon Volant. I had undertaken an adventure with a vengeance! And by way of prelude, there not improbably awaited me, at my inn, another encounter, perhaps, this time, not so lucky, with the grotesque sabreur.

I was glad I had my pistols. I certainly was bound by no law to allow a ruffian to cut me down, unresisting.

Stooping boughs from the old park, gigantic poplars on the other side, and the moonlight over all, made the narrow road to the inn-door picturesque.

I could not think very clearly just now; events were succeeding one another so rapidly, and I, involved in the action of a drama so extravagant and guilty, hardly knew myself or believed my own story, as I slowly paced towards the still open door of the Flying Dragon. No sign of the Colonel, visible or audible, was there. In the hall I inquired. No gentleman had arrived at the inn for the last half hour. I looked into the public room. It was deserted. The clock struck twelve, and I heard the servant barring the great door. I took my candle. The lights in this rural hostelry were by this time out, and the house had the air of one that had settled to slumber for many hours. The cold moonlight streamed in at the window on the landing as I ascended the broad staircase; and I paused for a moment to look over the wooded grounds to the turreted château, to me, so full of interest. I bethought me, however, that prying eyes might read a meaning in this midnight gazing, and possibly the Count himself might, in his jealous mood, surmise a signal in this unwonted light in the stair-window of the Dragon Volant.

On opening my room door, with a little start, I met an extremely old woman with the longest face I ever saw; she had what used to be termed a high-cauld-cap on, the white border of which contrasted with her brown and yellow skin, and made her wrinkled face more ugly. She raised her curved shoulders, and looked up in my face, with eyes unnaturally black and bright.

"I have lighted a little wood, Monsieur, because the night is chill."

I thanked her, but she did not go. She stood with her candle in her tremulous fingers.

"Excuse an old woman, Monsieur," she said; "but what on earth can a young English *milord*, with all Paris at his feet, find to amuse him in the Dragon Volant?"

Had I been at the age of fairy tales, and in daily intercourse with the delightful Countess d'Aulnois, I should have seen in this withered apparition, the genius loci, the malignant fairy, at the stamp of whose foot the ill-fated tenants of this very room had, from time to time, vanished. I was past that, however; but the old woman's dark eyes were fixed on mine with a steady meaning that plainly told me that my secret was known. I was embarrassed and alarmed; I never thought of asking her what business that was of hers.

"These old eyes saw you in the park of the château tonight."

"*I!*" I began, with all the scornful surprise I could affect.

"It avails nothing, Monsieur; I know why you stay here; and I tell you to begone. Leave this house tomorrow morning, and never come again."

She lifted her disengaged hand, as she looked at me with intense horror in her eyes.

"There is nothing on earth—I don't know what you mean," I answered, "and why should you care about me?"

"I don't care about you, Monsieur—I care about the honor of an ancient family, whom I served in their happier days, when to be noble was to be honored. But my words are thrown away, Monsieur; you are insolent. I will keep my secret, and you, yours; that is all. You will soon find it hard enough to divulge it."

The old woman went slowly from the room and shut the door, before I had made up my mind to say anything. I was standing where she had left me, nearly five minutes later. The jealousy of Monsieur the Count, I assumed, appears to this old creature about the most terrible thing in creation. Whatever contempt I might entertain for the dangers which this old lady so darkly intimated, it was by no means pleasant, you may suppose, that a secret so dangerous should be so much as suspected by a stranger, and that stranger a partisan of the Count de St. Alyre.

Ought I not, at all risks, to apprise the Countess, who had trusted me so generously, or, as she said herself, so madly, of the fact that our secret was, at least, suspected by another? But was there not greater danger in attempting to communicate? What did the beldame mean by saying, "Keep your secret, and I'll keep mine?"

I had a thousand distracting questions before me. My progress seemed like a journey through the Spessart, where at every step some new goblin or monster starts from the ground or steps from behind a tree.

Peremptorily I dismissed these harassing and frightful doubts. I secured my door, sat myself down at my table and, with a candle at each side, placed before me the piece of vellum which contained the drawings and notes on which I was to rely for full instructions as to how to use the key.

When I had studied this for awhile I made my investigation. The angle of the room at the right side of the window was cut off by an oblique turn in the wainscot. I examined this carefully, and, on pressure, a small bit of the frame of the woodwork slid aside, and disclosed a key-hole. On removing my finger, it shot back to its place again, with a spring. So far I had interpreted my instructions successfully. A similar search, next the door, and directly under this, was rewarded by a like discovery. The small end of the key fitted this, as it had the upper key-hole; and now, with two or three hard jerks at the key, a door in the panel opened, showing a strip of the bare wall and a narrow, arched doorway, piercing the thickness of the wall; and within which I saw a screw staircase of stone.

Candle in hand I stepped in. I do not know whether the quality of air, long undisturbed, is peculiar; to me it has always seemed so, and the damp smell of the old masonry hung in this atmosphere. My candle faintly lighted the bare stone wall that enclosed the stair, the foot of which I could not see. Down I went, and a few turns brought me to the stone floor. Here was another door, of the simple, old, oak kind, deep sunk in the thickness of the wall. The large end of the key fitted this. The lock was stiff; I set the candle down upon the stair, and applied both hands; it turned with difficulty and, as it revolved, uttered a shriek that alarmed me for my secret.

For some minutes I did not move. In a little time, however, I took courage, and opened the door. The night-air floating in puffed out the candle. There was a thicket of holly and underwood, as dense as a jungle, close about the door. I should have been in pitch-darkness, were it not that through the topmost leaves there twinkled, here and there, a glimmer of moonshine.

Softly, lest anyone should have opened his window at the sound of the rusty bolt, I struggled through this till I gained a view of the open grounds. Here I found that the brushwood spread a good way up the park, uniting with the wood that approached the little temple I have described.

A general could not have chosen a more effectually covered approach from the Dragon Volant to the trysting-place where hitherto I had conferred with the idol of my lawless adoration.

Looking back upon the old inn I discovered that the stair I descended was enclosed in one of those slender turrets that decorate such buildings. It was placed at that angle which corresponded with the part of the paneling of my room indicated in the plan I had been studying.

Thoroughly satisfied with my experiment I made my way back to the door with some little difficulty, remounted to my room, locked my secret door again; kissed the mysterious key that her hand had pressed that night, and placed it under my pillow, upon which, very soon after, my giddy head was laid, not, for some time, to sleep soundly.

CHAPTER TWENTY-ONE

I SEE THREE MEN IN A MIRROR

I awoke very early next morning, and was too excited to sleep again. As soon as I could, without exciting remark, I saw my host. I told him that I was going into town that night, and thence to ——, where I had to see some people on business, and requested him to mention my being there to any friend who might call. That I expected to be back in about a week, and that in the meantime my servant, St. Clair, would keep the key of my room and look after my things.

Having prepared this mystification for my landlord, I drove into Paris, and there transacted the financial part of the affair. The problem was to reduce my balance, nearly thirty thousand pounds, to a shape in which it would be not only easily portable, but available, wherever I might go, without involving correspondence, or any other incident which would disclose my place of residence for the time being. All these points were as nearly provided for as, they could be. I need not trouble you about my arrangements for passports. It is enough to say that the point I selected for our flight was, in the spirit of romance, one of the most beautiful and sequestered nooks in Switzerland.

Luggage, I should start with none. The first considerable town we reached next morning, would supply an extemporized wardrobe. It was now two o'clock; *only* two! How on earth was I to dispose of the remainder of the day?

I had not yet seen the cathedral of Notre Dame, and thither I drove. I spent an hour or more there; and then to the Conciergerie, the Palais de Justice, and the beautiful Sainte Chapelle. Still there remained some time to get rid of, and I strolled into the narrow streets adjoining the cathedral. I recollect seeing, in one of them, an old house with a mural inscription stating that it had been the residence of Canon Fulbert, the uncle of Abelard's Eloise. I don't know whether these curious old streets, in which I observed fragments of ancient Gothic churches fitted up as warehouses, are still extant. I lighted, among other dingy and eccentric shops, upon one that seemed that of a broker of all sorts of old decorations, armor, china, furniture. I entered the shop; it was dark, dusty, and low. The proprietor was busy scouring a piece of inlaid armor, and allowed me to poke about his shop, and examine the curious things accumulated there, just as I pleased. Gradually I made my way to the farther end of it, where there was but one window with many panes, each with a bull's eye in it, and in the dirtiest possible state. When I reached this window, I turned about, and in a recess, standing at right angles with the side wall of the shop, was a large mirror in an old-fashioned dingy frame. Reflected in this I saw what in old houses I have heard termed an "alcove," in which, among lumber and various dusty articles hanging on the wall, there stood a table, at which three persons were seated, as it seemed to me, in earnest conversation. Two of these persons I instantly recognized; one was Colonel Gaillarde, the other was the Marquis d'Harmonville. The third, who was fiddling with a pen, was a lean, pale man, pitted with the small-pox, with lank black hair, and about as mean-looking a person as I had ever seen in my life. The Marquis looked up, and his glance was instantaneously followed by his two companions. For a moment I hesitated what to do. But it was plain that I was not recognized, as indeed I could hardly have been, the light from the window being behind me, and the portion of the shop immediately before me being very dark indeed.

Perceiving this, I had presence of mind to affect being entirely engrossed by the objects before me, and strolled slowly down the shop again. I paused for a moment to hear whether I was followed, and was relieved when I heard no step. You may be sure I did not waste more time in that shop, where I had just made a discovery so curious and so unexpected.

It was no business of mine to inquire what brought Colonel Gaillarde and the Marquis together, in so shabby and even dirty a place, or who the mean person, biting the feather end of his pen, might be. Such employments as the Marquis had accepted sometimes make strange bedfellows.

I was glad to get away, and just as the sun set I had reached the steps of the Dragon Volant, and dismissed the vehicle in which I arrived, carrying in my hand a strong box, of marvelously small dimensions considering all it contained, strapped in a leather cover which disguised its real character.

When I got to my room I summoned St. Clair. I told him nearly the same story I had already told my host. I gave him fifty pounds, with orders to expend whatever was necessary on himself, and in payment for my rooms till my return. I then ate a slight and hasty dinner. My eyes were often upon the solemn old clock over the chimney-piece, which was my sole accomplice in keeping tryst in this iniquitous venture. The sky favored my design, and darkened all things with a sea of clouds.

The innkeeper met me in the hall, to ask whether I should want a vehicle to Paris? I was prepared for this question, and instantly answered that I meant to walk to Versailles and take a carriage there. I called St. Clair.

"Go," said I, "and drink a bottle of wine with your friends. I shall call you if I should want anything; in the meantime, here is the key to my room; I shall be writing some notes, so don't allow anyone to disturb me for at least half an hour. At the end of that time you will probably find that I have left this for Versailles; and should you not find me in the room, you may take that for granted; and you take charge of everything, and lock the door, you understand?"

St. Clair took his leave, wishing me all happiness, and no doubt promising himself some little amusement with my money. With my candle in my hand, I hastened upstairs. It wanted now but five minutes to the appointed time. I do not think there is anything of the coward in my nature; but I confess, as the crisis approached, I felt something of the suspense and awe of a soldier going into action. Would I have receded? Not for all this earth could offer.

I bolted my door, put on my greatcoat, and placed my pistols one in each pocket. I now applied my key to the secret locks; drew the wainscot door a little open, took my strong box under my arm, extinguished my candle, unbolted my door, listened at it for a few moments to be sure that no one was approaching, and then crossed the floor of my room swiftly, entered the secret door, and closed the spring lock after me. I was upon the screw-stair in total darkness, the key in my fingers. Thus far the undertaking was successful.

CHAPTER TWENTY-TWO

RAPTURE

Down the screw-stair I went in utter darkness; and having reached the stone floor I discerned the door and groped out the key-hole. With more caution, and less noise than upon the night before, I opened the door and stepped out into the thick brushwood. It was almost as dark in this jungle.

Having secured the door I slowly pushed my way through the bushes, which soon became less dense. Then, with more case, but still under thick cover, I pursued in the track of the wood, keeping near its edge.

At length, in the darkened air, about fifty yards away, the shafts of the marble temple rose like phantoms before me, seen through the trunks of the old trees. Everything favored my enterprise. I had effectually mystified my servant and the people of the Dragon Volant, and so dark was the night, that even had I alarmed the suspicions of all the tenants of the inn, I might safely defy their united curiosity, though posted at every window of the house.

Through the trunks, over the roots of the old trees, I reached the appointed place of observation. I laid my treasure in its leathern case in the embrasure, and leaning my arms upon it, looked steadily in the direction of the château. The outline of the building was scarcely discernible, blending dimly, as it did, with the sky. No light in any window was visible. I was plainly to wait; but for how long?

Leaning on my box of treasure, gazing toward the massive shadow that represented the château, in the midst of my ardent and elated longings, there came upon me an odd thought, which you will think might well have struck me long before. It seemed on a sudden, as it came, that the darkness deepened, and a chill stole into the air around me.

Suppose I were to disappear finally, like those other men whose stories I had listened to! Had I not been at all the pains that mortal could to obliterate every trace of my real proceedings, and to mislead everyone to whom I spoke as to the direction in which I had gone?

This icy, snake-like thought stole through my mind, and was gone.

It was with me the full-blooded season of youth, conscious strength, rashness, passion, pursuit, the adventure! Here were a pair of double-barreled pistols, four lives in my hands? What could possibly happen? The Count—except for the sake of my dulcinea, what was it to me whether the old coward whom I had seen, in an ague of terror before the brawling Colonel, interposed or not? I was assuming the worst that could happen. But with an ally so clever and courageous as my beautiful Countess, could any such misadventure befall? Bah! I laughed at all such fancies.

As I thus communed with myself, the signal light sprang up. The rose-colored light, *couleur de rose,* emblem of sanguine hope and the dawn of a happy day.

Clear, soft, and steady, glowed the light from the window. The stone shafts showed black against it. Murmuring words of passionate love as I gazed upon the signal, I grasped my strong box under my arm, and with rapid strides approached the Château de la Carque. No sign of light or life, no human voice, no tread of foot, no bark of dog indicated a chance of interruption. A blind was down; and as I came close to the tall window, I found that half-a-dozen steps led up to it, and that a large lattice, answering for a door, lay open.

A shadow from within fell upon the blind; it was drawn aside, and as I ascended the steps, a soft voice murmured—"Richard, dearest Richard, come, oh! come! how I have longed for this moment!"

Never did she look so beautiful. My love rose to passionate enthusiasm. I only wished there were some real danger in the adventure worthy of such a creature. When the first tumultuous greeting was over, she made me sit beside her on a sofa. There we talked for a minute or two. She told me that the Count had gone, and was by that time more than a mile on his way, with the funeral, to Père la Chaise. Here were her diamonds. She exhibited, hastily, an open casket containing a profusion of the largest brilliants.

"What is this?" she asked.

"A box containing money to the amount of thirty thousand pounds," I answered.

"What! all that money?" she exclaimed.

"Every sou."

"Was it not unnecessary to bring so much, seeing all these?" she said, touching her diamonds. "It would have been kind of you to allow me to provide for both, for a time at least. It would have made me happier even than I am."

"Dearest, generous angel!" Such was my extravagant declamation. "You forget that it may be necessary, for a long time, to observe silence as to where we are, and impossible to communicate safely with anyone."

"You have then here this great sum—are you certain; have you counted it?"

"Yes, certainly; I received it today," I answered, perhaps showing a little surprise in my face. "I counted it, of course, on drawing it from my bankers."

"It makes me feel a little nervous, traveling with so much money; but these jewels make as great a danger; that can add but little to it. Place them side by side; you shall take off your greatcoat when we are ready to go, and with it manage to conceal these boxes. I should not like the drivers to suspect that we were conveying such a treasure. I must ask you now to close the curtains of that window, and bar the shutters."

I had hardly done this when a knock was heard at the room door.

"I know who this is," she said, in a whisper to me.

I saw that she was not alarmed. She went softly to the door, and a whispered conversation for a minute followed.

"My trusty maid, who is coming with us. She says we cannot safely go sooner than ten minutes. She is bringing some coffee to the next room."

She opened the door and looked in.

"I must tell her not to take too much luggage. She is so odd! Don't follow—stay where you are—it is better that she should not see you."

She left the room with a gesture of caution.

A change had come over the manner of this beautiful woman. For the last few minutes a shadow had been stealing over her, an air of abstraction, a look bordering on suspicion. Why was she pale? Why had there come that dark look in her eyes? Why had her very voice become changed? Had anything gone suddenly wrong? Did some danger threaten?

This doubt, however, speedily quieted itself. If there had been anything of the kind, she would, of course, have told me. It was only natural that, as the crisis approached, she should become more and more nervous. She did not return quite so soon as I had expected. To a man in my situation absolute quietude is next to impossible. I moved restlessly about the room. It was a small one. There was a door at the other end. I opened it, rashly enough. I listened, it was perfectly silent. I was in an excited, eager state, and every faculty engrossed about what was coming, and in so far detached from the immediate present. I can't account, in any other way, for my having done so many foolish things that night, for I was, naturally, by no means deficient in cunning. About the most stupid of those was, that instead of immediately closing that door, which I never ought to have opened, I actually took a candle and walked into the room.

There I made, quite unexpectedly, a rather startling discovery.

CHAPTER TWENTY-THREE

A CUP OF COFFEE

The room was carpetless. On the floor were a quantity of shavings, and some score of bricks. Beyond these, on a narrow table, lay an object which I could hardly believe I saw aright.

I approached and drew from it a sheet which had very slightly disguised its shape. There was no mistake about it. It was a coffin; and on the lid was a plate, with the inscription in French:

PIERRE DE LA ROCHE ST. AMAND.
ÂGÉ DE XXIII ANS.

I drew back with a double shock. So, then, the funeral after all had not yet left! Here lay the body. I had been deceived. This, no doubt, accounted for the embarrassment so manifest in the Countess's manner. She would have done more wisely had she told me the true state of the case.

I drew back from this melancholy room, and closed the door. Her distrust of me was the worst rashness she could have committed. There is nothing more dangerous than misapplied caution. In entire ignorance of the fact I had entered the room, and there I might have lighted upon some of the very persons it was our special anxiety that I should avoid.

These reflections were interrupted, almost as soon as began, by the return of the Countess de St. Alyre. I saw at a glance that she detected in my face some evidence of what had happened, for she threw a hasty look towards the door.

"Have you seen anything—anything to disturb you, dear Richard? Have you been out of this room?"

I answered promptly, "Yes," and told her frankly what had happened.

"Well, I did not like to make you more uneasy than necessary. Besides, it is disgusting and horrible. The body is there; but the Count had departed a quarter of an hour before I lighted the colored lamp, and prepared to receive you. The body did not arrive till eight or ten minutes after he had set out. He was afraid lest the people at Père la Chaise should suppose that the funeral was postponed. He knew that the remains of poor Pierre would certainly reach this tonight, although an unexpected delay has occurred; and there are reasons why he wishes the funeral completed before tomorrow. The hearse with the body must leave this in ten minutes. So soon as it is gone, we shall be free to set out upon our wild and happy journey. The horses are to the carriage in the *porte-cochère*. As for this *funeste* horror" (she shuddered very prettily), "let us think of it no more."

She bolted the door of communication, and when she turned it was with such a pretty penitence in her face and attitude, that I was ready to throw myself at her feet.

"It is the last time," she said, in a sweet sad little pleading, "I shall ever practice a deception on my brave and beautiful Richard—my hero! Am I forgiven?"

Here was another scene of passionate effusion, and lovers' raptures and declamations, but only murmured lest the ears of listeners should be busy.

At length, on a sudden, she raised her hand, as if to prevent my stirring, her eyes fixed on me and her ear toward the door of the room in which the coffin was placed, and remained breathless in that attitude for a few moments. Then, with a little nod towards me, she moved on tiptoe to the door, and listened, extending her hand backward as if to warn me against advancing; and, after a little time, she returned, still on tiptoe, and whispered to me, "They are removing the coffin—come with me."

I accompanied her into the room from which her maid, as she told me, had spoken to her. Coffee and some old china cups, which appeared to me quite beautiful, stood on a silver tray; and some liqueur glasses, with a flask, which turned out to be noyau, on a salver beside it.

"I shall attend you. I'm to be your servant here; I am to have my own way; I shall not think myself forgiven by my darling if he refuses to indulge me in anything."

She filled a cup with coffee and handed it to me with her left hand; her right arm she fondly passed over my shoulder, and with her fingers through my curls, caressingly, she whispered, "Take this, I shall take some just now."

It was excellent; and when I had done she handed me the liqueur, which I also drank.

"Come back, dearest, to the next room," she said. "By this time those terrible people must have gone away, and we shall be safer there, for the present, than here."

"You shall direct, and I obey; you shall command me, not only now, but always, and in all things, my beautiful queen!" I murmured.

My heroics were unconsciously, I daresay, founded upon my ideal of the French school of lovemaking. I am, even now, ashamed as I recall the bombast to which I treated the Countess de St. Alyre.

"There, you shall have another miniature glass—a fairy glass—of noyau," she said gaily. In this volatile creature, the funereal gloom of the moment before, and the suspense of an adventure on which all her future was staked, disappeared in a moment. She ran and returned with another tiny glass, which, with an eloquent or tender little speech, I placed to my lips and sipped.

I kissed her hand, I kissed her lips, I gazed in her beautiful eyes, and kissed her again unresisting.

"You call me Richard, by what name am I to call my beautiful divinity?" I asked.

"You call me Eugenie, it is my name. Let us be quite real; that is, if you love as entirely as I do."

"Eugenie!" I exclaimed, and broke into a new rapture upon the name.

It ended by my telling her how impatient I was to set out upon our journey; and, as I spoke, suddenly an odd sensation overcame me. It was not in the slightest degree like faintness. I can find no phrase to describe it, but a sudden constraint of the brain; it was as if the membrane in which it lies, if there be such a thing, contracted, and became inflexible.

"Dear Richard! what is the matter?" she exclaimed, with terror in her looks. "Good Heavens! are you ill? I conjure you, sit down; sit in this chair." She almost forced me into one; I was in no condition to offer the least resistance. I recognized but too truly the sensations that supervened. I was lying back in the chair in which I sat, without the power, by this time, of uttering a syllable, of closing my eyelids, of moving my eyes, of stirring a muscle. I had in a few seconds glided into precisely the state in which I had passed so many appalling hours when approaching Paris, in my night-drive with the Marquis d'Harmonville.

Great and loud was the lady's agony. She seemed to have lost all sense of fear. She called me by my name, shook me by the shoulder, raised my arm and let it fall, all the time imploring of me, in distracting sentences, to make the slightest sign of life, and vowing that if I did not, she would make away with herself.

These ejaculations, after a minute or two, suddenly subsided. The lady was perfectly silent and cool. In a very business-like way she took a candle and stood before me, pale indeed, very pale, but with an expression only of intense scrutiny with a dash of horror in it. She moved the candle before my eyes slowly, evidently watching the effect. She then set it down, and rang a handball two or three times sharply. She placed the two cases (I mean hers containing the jewels and my strong box) side by side on the table; and I saw her carefully lock the door that gave access to the room in which I had just now sipped my coffee.

CHAPTER TWENTY-FOUR

HOPE

She had scarcely set down my heavy box, which she seemed to have considerable difficulty in raising on the table, when the door of the room in which I had seen the coffin, opened, and a sinister and unexpected apparition entered.

It was the Count de St. Alyre, who had been, as I have told you, reported to me to be, for some considerable time, on his way to Pèe la Chaise. He stood before me for a moment, with the frame of the doorway and a background of darkness enclosing him like a portrait. His slight, mean figure was draped in the deepest mourning. He had a pair of black gloves in his hand, and his hat with crape round it.

When he was not speaking his face showed signs of agitation; his mouth was puckering and working. He looked damnably wicked and frightened.

"Well, my dear Eugenie? Well, child—eh? Well, it all goes admirably?"

"Yes," she answered, in a low, hard tone. "But you and Planard should not have left that door open."

This she said sternly. "He went in there and looked about wherever he liked; it was fortunate he did not move aside the lid of the coffin."

"Planard should have seen to that," said the Count, sharply. *"Ma foi! I can't be everywhere!"* He advanced half-a-dozen short quick steps into the room toward me, and placed his glasses to his eyes.

"Monsieur Beckett," he cried sharply, two or three times, "Hi! Don't you know me?"

He approached and peered more closely in my face; raised my hand and shook it, calling me again, then let it drop, and said: "It has set in admirably, my pretty *mignonne.* When did it commence?"

The Countess came and stood beside him, and looked at me steadily for some seconds. You can't conceive the effect of the silent gaze of those two pairs of evil eyes.

The lady glanced to where, I recollected, the mantel piece stood, and upon it a clock, the regular click of which I sharply heard. "Four—five—six minutes and a half," she said slowly, in a cold hard way.

"Brava! Bravissima! my beautiful queen! my little Venus! my Joan of Arc! my heroine! my paragon of women!"

He was gloating on me with an odious curiosity, smiling, as he groped backward with his thin brown fingers to find the lady's hand; but she, not (I dare say) caring for his caresses, drew back a little.

"Come, *ma chère,* let us count these things. What is it? Pocket-book? Or—or—*what*?"

"It is *that*!" said the lady, pointing with a look of disgust to the box, which lay in its leather case on the table.

"Oh! Let us see—let us count—let us see," he said, as he was unbuckling the straps with his tremulous fingers. "We must count them—we must see to it. I have pencil and pocket-book—but—where's the key? See this cursed lock! My—! What is it? Where's the key?"

He was standing before the Countess, shuffling his feet, with his hands extended and all his fingers quivering.

"I have not got it; how could I? It is in his pocket, of course," said the lady.

In another instant the fingers of the old miscreant were in my pockets; he plucked out everything they contained, and some keys among the rest.

I lay in precisely the state in which I had been during my drive with the Marquis to Paris. This wretch, I knew, was about to rob me. The whole drama, and the Countess's *rôle* in it, I could not yet comprehend. I could not be sure—so much more presence of mind and histrionic resource have women than fall to the lot of our clumsy sex—whether the return of the Count was not, in truth, a surprise to her; and this scrutiny of the contents of my strong box, an extempore undertaking of the Count's. But it was clearing more and more every moment: and I was destined, very soon, to comprehend minutely my appalling situation.

I had not the power of turning my eyes this way or that, the smallest fraction of a hair's breadth. But let anyone, placed as I was at the end of a room, ascertain for himself by experiment how wide is the field of sight, without the slightest alteration in the line of vision, he will find that it takes in the entire breadth of a large room, and that up to a very short distance before him; and imperfectly, by a refraction, I believe, in the eye itself, to a point very near indeed. Next to nothing that passed in the room, therefore, was hidden from me.

The old man had, by this time, found the key. The leather case was open. The box cramped round with iron was next unlocked. He turned out its contents upon the table.

"Rouleaux of a hundred Napoleons each. One, two, three. Yes, quick. Write down a thousand Napoleons. One, two; yes, right. Another thousand, *write*!" And so on and on till the gold was rapidly counted. Then came the notes.

"Ten thousand francs. *Write*. Then thousand francs again. Is it written? Another ten thousand francs: is it down? Smaller notes would have been better. They should have been smaller. These are horribly embarrassing. Bolt that door again; Planard would become unreasonable if he knew the amount. Why did you not tell him to get it in smaller notes? No matter now—go on—it can't be helped—*write*—another ten thousand francs—another—another." And so on, till my treasure was counted out before my face, while I saw and heard all that passed with the sharpest distinctness, and my mental perceptions were horribly vivid. But in all other respects I was dead.

He had replaced in the box every note and rouleau as he counted it, and now, having ascertained the sum total, he locked it, replaced it very methodically in its cover, opened a buffet in the wainscoting, and, having placed the Countess' jewel-case and my strong box in it, he locked it; and immediately on completing these arrangements he began to complain, with fresh acrimony and maledictions of Planard's delay.

He unbolted the door, looked in the dark room beyond, and listened. He closed the door again and returned. The old man was in a fever of suspense.

"I have kept ten thousand francs for Planard," said the Count, touching his waistcoat pocket.

"Will that satisfy him?" asked the lady.

"Why—curse him!" screamed the Count. "Has he no conscience? I'll swear to him it's half the entire thing."

He and the lady again came and looked at me anxiously for a while, in silence; and then the old Count began to grumble again about Planard, and to compare his watch with the clock. The lady seemed less impatient; she sat no longer looking at me, but across the room, so that her profile was toward me—and strangely changed, dark and witch-like it looked. My last hope died as I beheld that jaded face from which the mask had dropped. I was certain that they intended to crown their robbery by murder. Why did they not dispatch me at once? What object could there be in postponing the catastrophe which would expedite their own safety. I cannot recall, even to myself, adequately the horrors unutterable that I underwent. You must suppose a real night-mare—I mean a night-mare in which the objects and the danger are real, and the spell of corporal death appears to be protractible at the pleasure of the persons who preside at your unearthly torments. I could have no doubt as to the cause of the state in which I was.

In this agony, to which I could not give the slightest expression, I saw the door of the room where the coffin had been, open slowly, and the Marquis d'Harmonville entered the room.

CHAPTER TWENTY-FIVE

DESPAIR

A moment's hope, hope violent and fluctuating, hope that was nearly torture, and then came a dialogue, and with it the terrors of despair.

"Thank Heaven, Planard, you have come at last," said the Count, taking him with both hands by the arm, and clinging to it and drawing him toward me. "See, look at him. It has all gone sweetly, sweetly, sweetly up to this. Shall I hold the candle for you?"

My friend d'Harmonville, Planard, whatever he was, came to me, pulling off his gloves, which he popped into his pocket.

"The candle, a little this way," he said, and stooping over me he looked earnestly in my face. He touched my forehead, drew his hand across it, and then looked in my eyes for a time.

"Well, doctor, what do you think?" whispered the Count.

"How much did you give him?" said the Marquis, thus suddenly stunted down to a doctor.

"Seventy drops," said the lady.

"In the hot coffee?"

"Yes; sixty in a hot cup of coffee and ten in the liqueur."

Her voice, low and hard, seemed to me to tremble a little. It takes a long course of guilt to subjugate nature completely, and prevent those exterior signs of agitation that outlive all good.

The doctor, however, was treating me as coolly as he might a subject which he was about to place on the dissecting-table for a lecture.

He looked into my eyes again for awhile, took my wrist, and applied his fingers to the pulse.

"That action suspended," he said to himself.

Then again he placed something, that for the moment I saw it looked like a piece of gold-beater's leaf, to my lips, holding his head so far that his own breathing could not affect it.

"Yes," he said in soliloquy, very low.

Then he plucked my shirt-breast open and applied the stethoscope, shifted it from point to point, listened with his ear to its end, as if for a very far-off sound, raised his head, and said, in like manner, softly to himself, "All appreciable action of the lungs has subsided."

Then turning from the sound, as I conjectured, he said:

"Seventy drops, allowing ten for waste, ought to hold him fast for six hours and a half-that is ample. The experiment I tried in the carriage was only thirty drops, and showed a highly sensitive brain. It would not do to kill him, you know. You are certain you did not exceed *seventy*?"

"Perfectly," said the lady.

"If he were to die the evaporation would be arrested, and foreign matter, some of it poisonous, would be found in the stomach, don't you see? If you are doubtful, it would be well to use the stomach-pump."

"Dearest Eugenie, be frank, be frank, do be frank," urged the Count.

"I am *not* doubtful, I am *certain*," she answered.

"How long ago, exactly? I told you to observe the time."

"I did; the minute-hand was exactly there, under the point of that Cupid's foot."

"It will last, then, probably for seven hours. He will recover then; the evaporation will be complete, and not one particle of the fluid will remain in the stomach."

It was reassuring, at all events, to hear that there was no intention to murder me. No one who has not tried it knows the terror of the approach of death, when the mind is clear, the instincts of life unimpaired, and no excitement to disturb the appreciation of that entirely new horror.

The nature and purpose of this tenderness was very, very peculiar, and as yet I had not a suspicion of it.

"You leave France, I suppose?" said the ex-Marquis.

"Yes, certainly, tomorrow," answered the Count.

"And where do you mean to go?"

"That I have not yet settled," he answered quickly.

"You won't tell a friend, eh?"

"I can't till I know. This has turned out an unprofitable affair."

"We shall settle that by-and-by."

"It is time we should get him lying down, eh," said the Count, indicating me with one finger.

"Yes, we must proceed rapidly now. Are his night-shirt and night-cap—you understand—here?"

"All ready," said the Count.

"Now, Madame," said the doctor, turning to the lady, and making her, in spite of the emergency, a bow, "it is time you should retire."

The lady passed into the room in which I had taken my cup of treacherous coffee, and I saw her no more. The Count took a candle and passed through the door at the further end of the room, returning with a roll of linen in his hand. He bolted first one door then the other.

They now, in silence, proceeded to undress me rapidly. They were not many minutes in accomplishing this.

What the doctor had termed my night-shirt, a long garment which reached below my feet, was now on, and a cap, that resembled a female nightcap more than anything I had ever seen upon a male head, was fitted upon mine, and tied under my chin.

And now, I thought, I shall be laid in a bed to recover how I can, and, in the meantime, the conspirators will have escaped with their booty, and pursuit be in vain.

This was my best hope at the time; but it was soon clear that their plans were very different. The Count and Planard now went, together, into the room that lay straight before me. I heard them talking low, and a sound of shuffling feet; then a long rumble; it suddenly stopped; it re-commenced; it continued; side by side they came in at the door, their backs toward me. They were dragging something along the floor that made a continued boom and rumble, but they interposed between me and it, so that I could not see it until they had dragged it almost beside me; and then, merciful heaven! I saw it plainly enough. It was the coffin I had seen in the next room. It lay now flat on the floor, its edge against the chair in which I sat. Planard removed the lid. The coffin was empty.

CHAPTER TWENTY-SIX

CATASTROPHE

"Those seem to be good horses, and we change on the way," said Planard. "You give the men a Napoleon or two; we must do it within three hours and a quarter. Now, come; I'll lift him upright, so as to place his feet in their proper berth, and you must keep them together and draw the white shirt well down over them."

In another moment I was placed, as he described, sustained in Planard's arms, standing at the foot of the coffin, and so lowered backward, gradually, till I lay my length in it. Then the man, whom he called Planard, stretched my arms by my sides, and carefully arranged the frills at my breast and the folds of the shroud, and after that, taking his stand at the foot of the coffin made a survey which seemed to satisfy him.

The Count, who was very methodical, took my clothes, which had just been removed, folded them rapidly together and locked them up, as I afterwards heard, in one of the three presses which opened by doors in the panel.

I now understood their frightful plan. This coffin had been prepared for me; the funeral of St. Amand was a sham to mislead inquiry; I had myself given the order at Père la Chaise, signed it, and paid the fees for the interment of the fictitious Pierre de St. Amand, whose place I was to take, to lie in his coffin with his name on the plate above my breast, and with a ton of clay packed down upon me; to waken from this catalepsy, after I had been for hours in the grave, there to perish by a death the most horrible that imagination can conceive.

If, hereafter, by any caprice of curiosity or suspicion, the coffin should be exhumed, and the body it enclosed examined, no chemistry could detect a trace of poison, nor the most cautious examination the slightest mark of violence.

I had myself been at the utmost pains to mystify inquiry, should my disappearance excite surmises, and had even written to my few correspondents in England to tell them that they were not to look for a letter from me for three weeks at least.

In the moment of my guilty elation death had caught me, and there was no escape. I tried to pray to God in my unearthly panic, but only thoughts of terror, judgment, and eternal anguish crossed the distraction of my immediate doom.

I must not try to recall what is indeed indescribable—the multiform horrors of my own thoughts. I will relate, simply, what befell, every detail of which remains sharp in my memory as if cut in steel.

"The undertaker's men are in the hall," said the Count.

"They must not come till this is fixed," answered Planard. "Be good enough to take hold of the lower part while I take this end." I was not left long to conjecture what was coming, for in a few seconds more something slid across, a few inches above my face, and entirely excluded the light, and muffled sound, so that nothing that was not very distinct reached my ears henceforward; but very distinctly came the working of a turnscrew, and the crunching home of screws in succession. Than these vulgar sounds, no doom spoken in thunder could have been more tremendous.

The rest I must relate, not as it then reached my ears, which was too imperfectly and interruptedly to supply a connected narrative, but as it was afterwards told me by other people.

The coffin-lid being screwed down, the two gentlemen arranged the room and adjusted the coffin so that it lay perfectly straight along the boards, the Count being specially anxious that there should be no appearance of hurry or disorder in the room, which might have suggested remark and conjecture.

When this was done, Doctor Planard said he would go to the hall to summon the men who were to carry the coffin out and place it in the hearse. The Count pulled on his black gloves, and held his white handkerchief in his hand, a very impressive chief-mourner. He stood a little behind the head of the coffin, awaiting the arrival of the persons who accompanied Planard, and whose fast steps he soon heard approaching.

Planard came first. He entered the room through the apartment in which the coffin had been originally placed. His manner was changed; there was something of a swagger in it.

"Monsieur le Comte," he said, as he strode through the door, followed by half-a-dozen persons, "I am sorry to have to announce to you a most unseasonable interruption. Here is Monsieur Carmaignac, a gentleman holding an office in the police department, who says that information to the effect that large quantities of smuggled English and other goods have been distributed in this neighborhood, and that a portion of them is concealed in your house. I have ventured to assure him, of my own knowledge, that nothing can be more false than that information, and that you would be only too happy to throw open for his inspection, at a moment's notice, every room, closet, and cupboard in your house."

"Most assuredly," exclaimed the Count, with a stout voice, but a very white face. "Thank you, my good friend, for having anticipated me. I will place my house and keys at his disposal, for the purpose of his scrutiny, so soon as he is good enough to inform me of what specific contraband goods he comes in search."

"The Count de St. Alyre will pardon me," answered Carmaignac, a little dryly. "I *am* forbidden by my instructions to make that disclosure; and that I am instructed to make a general search, this warrant will sufficiently apprise Monsieur le Comte."

"Monsieur Carmaignac, may I hope," interposed Planard, "that you will permit the Count de St. Alyre to attend the funeral of his kinsman, who lies here, as you see—" (he pointed to the plate upon the coffin)—"and to convey whom to Pere la Chaise, a hearse waits at this moment at the door."

"That, I regret to say, I cannot permit. My instructions are precise; but the delay, I trust, will be but trifling. Monsieur le Comte will not suppose for a moment that I suspect him; but we have a duty to perform, and I must act as if I did. When I am ordered to search, I search; things are sometimes hid in such bizarre places. I can't say, for instance, what that coffin may contain."

"The body of my kinsman, Monsieur Pierre de St. Amand," answered the Count, loftily.

"Oh! then you've seen him?"

"Seen him? Often, too often." The Count was evidently a good deal moved.

"I mean the body?"

The Count stole a quick glance at Planard.

"N—no, Monsieur—that is, I mean only for a moment."

Another quick glance at Planard.

"But quite long enough, I fancy, to recognize him?" insinuated that gentleman.

"Of course—of course; instantly—perfectly. What! Pierre de St. Amand? Not know him at a glance? No, no, poor fellow, I know him too well for that."

"The things I am in search of," said Monsieur Carmaignac, "would fit in a narrow compass—servants are so ingenious sometimes. Let us raise the lid."

"Pardon me, Monsieur," said the Count, peremptorily, advancing to the side of the coffin and extending his arm across it, "I cannot permit that indignity—that desecration."

"There shall be none, sir—simply the raising of the lid; you shall remain in the room. If it should prove as we all hope, you shall have the pleasure of one other look, really the last, upon your beloved kinsman."

"But, sir, I can't."

"But, Monsieur, I must."

"But, besides, the thing, the turnscrew, broke when the last screw was turned; and I give you my sacred honor there is nothing but the body in this coffin."

"Of course, Monsieur le Comte believes all that; but he does not know so well as I the legerdemain in use among servants, who are accustomed to smuggling. Here, Philippe, you must take off the lid of that coffin."

The Count protested; but Philippe—a man with a bald head and a smirched face, looking like a working blacksmith—placed on the floor a leather bag of tools, from which, having looked at the coffin, and picked with his nail at the screw-heads, he selected a turnscrew and, with a few deft twirls at each of the screws, they stood up like little rows of mushrooms, and the lid was raised. I saw the light, of which I thought I had seen my last, once more; but the axis of vision remained fixed. As I was reduced to the cataleptic state in a position nearly perpendicular, I continued looking straight before me, and thus my gaze was now fixed upon the ceiling. I saw the face of Carmaignac leaning over me with a curious frown. It seemed to me that there was no recognition in his eyes. Oh, Heaven! that I could have uttered were it but one cry! I saw the dark, mean mask of the little Count staring down at me from the other side; the face of the pseudo-Marquis also peering at me, but not so full in the line of vision; there were other faces also.

"I see, I see," said Carmaignac, withdrawing. "Nothing of the kind there."

"You will be good enough to direct your man to readjust the lid of the coffin, and to fix the screws," said the Count, taking courage; "and—

and—really the funeral must proceed. It is not fair to the people, who have but moderate fees for night-work, to keep them hour after hour beyond the time."

"Count de St. Alyre, you shall go in a very few minutes. I will direct, just now, all about the coffin."

The Count looked toward the door, and there saw a *gendarme*; and two or three more grave and stalwart specimens of the same force were also in the room. The Count was very uncomfortably excited; it was growing insupportable.

"As this gentleman makes a difficulty about my attending the obsequies of my kinsman, I will ask you, Planard, to accompany the funeral in my stead."

"In a few minutes;" answered the incorrigible Carmaignac. "I must first trouble you for the key that opens that press."

He pointed direct at the press in which the clothes had just been locked up.

"I—I have no objection," said the Count—"none, of course; only they have not been used for an age. I'll direct someone to look for the key."

"If you have not got it about you, it is quite unnecessary. Philippe, try your skeleton-keys with that press. I want it opened. Whose clothes are these?" inquired Carmaignac, when, the press having been opened, he took out the suit that had been placed there scarcely two minutes since.

"I can't say," answered the Count. "I know nothing of the contents of that press. A roguish servant, named Lablais, whom I dismissed about a year ago, had the key. I have not seen it open for ten years or more. The clothes are probably his."

"Here are visiting cards, see, and here a marked pocket-handkerchief—'R.B.' upon it. He must have stolen them from a person named Beckett—R. Beckett. 'Mr. Beckett, Berkeley Square,' the card says; and, my faith! Here's a watch and a bunch of seals; one of them with the initials 'R.B.' upon it. That servant, Lablais, must have been a consummate rogue!"

"So he was; you are right, Sir."

"It strikes me that he possibly stole these clothes," continued Carmaignac, "from the man in the coffin, who, in that case, would be Monsieur Beckett, and not Monsieur de St. Amand. For wonderful to relate, Monsieur, the watch is still going! The man in the coffin, I believe, is not dead, but simply drugged. And for having robbed and intended to murder him, I arrest you, Nicolas de la Marque, Count de St. Alyre."

In another moment the old villain was a prisoner. I heard his discordant voice break quaveringly into sudden vehemence and volubility; now croaking—now shrieking as he oscillated between protests, threats, and impious appeals to the God who will "judge the secrets of men!" And thus lying and raving, he was removed from the room, and placed in the same coach with his beautiful and abandoned accomplice, already arrested; and, with two *gendarmes* sitting beside them, they were immediate driving at a rapid pace towards the Conciergerie.

There were now added to the general chorus two voices, very different in quality; one was that of the gasconading Colonel Gaillarde, who had with difficulty been kept in the background up to this; the other was that of my jolly friend Whistlewick, who had come to identify me.

I shall tell you, just now, how this project against my property and life, so ingenious and monstrous, was exploded. I must first say a word about myself. I was placed in a hot bath, under the direction of Planard, as consummate a villain as any of the gang, but now thoroughly in the interests of the prosecution. Thence I was laid in a warm bed, the window of the room being open. These simple measures restored me in about three hours; I should otherwise, probably, have continued under the spell for nearly seven.

The practices of these nefarious conspirators had been carried on with consummate skill and secrecy. Their dupes were led, as I was, to be themselves auxiliary to the mystery which made their own destruction both safe and certain.

A search was, of course, instituted. Graves were opened in Pere la Chaise. The bodies exhumed had lain there too long, and were too much decomposed to be recognized. One only was identified. The notice for the burial, in this particular case, had been signed, the order given, and the fees paid, by Gabriel Gaillarde, who was known to the official clerk, who had to transact with him this little funereal business. The very trick that had been arranged for me, had been successfully practiced in his case. The person for whom the grave had been ordered, was purely fictitious; and Gabriel Gaillarde himself filled the coffin, on the cover of which that false name was inscribed as well as upon a tomb-stone over the grave. Possibly the same honor, under my pseudonym, may have been intended for me.

The identification was curious. This Gabriel Gaillarde had had a bad fall from a runaway horse about five years before his mysterious disappearance. He had lost an eye and some teeth in this accident, beside sustaining a fracture of the right leg, immediately above the ankle. He had kept the injuries to his face as profound a secret as he could. The result was, that the glass eye which had done duty for the one he had lost remained in the socket, slightly displaced, of course, but recognizable by the "artist" who had supplied it.

More pointedly recognizable were the teeth, peculiar in workmanship, which one of the ablest dentists in Paris had himself adapted to the chasms, the cast of which, owing to peculiarities in the accident, he happened to have preserved. This cast precisely fitted the gold plate found in the mouth of the skull. The mark, also, above the ankle, in the bone, where it had reunited, corresponded exactly with the place where the fracture had knit in the limb of Gabriel Gaillarde.

The Colonel, his younger brother, had been furious about the disappearance of Gabriel, and still more so about that of his money, which he had long regarded as his proper keepsake, whenever death should remove his brother from the vexations of living. He had suspected for a long time, for certain adroitly discovered reasons, that the Count de St.

Alyre and the beautiful lady, his companion, countess, or whatever else she was, had pigeoned him. To this suspicion were added some others of a still darker kind; but in their first shape, rather the exaggerated reflections of his fury, ready to believe anything, than well-defined conjectures.

At length an accident had placed the Colonel very nearly upon the right scent; a chance, possibly lucky, for himself, had apprised the scoundrel Planard that the conspirators—himself among the number—were in danger. The result was that he made terms for himself, became an informer, and concerted with the police this visit made to the Château de la Carque at the critical moment when every measure had been completed that was necessary to construct a perfect case against his guilty accomplices.

I need not describe the minute industry or forethought with which the police agents collected all the details necessary to support the case. They had brought an able physician, who, even had Planard failed, would have supplied the necessary medical evidence.

My trip to Paris, you will believe, had not turned out quite so agreeably as I had anticipated. I was the principal witness for the prosecution in this cause célèbre, with all the agrémens that attend that enviable position. Having had an escape, as my friend Whistlewick said, "with a squeak" for my life, I innocently fancied that I should have been an object of considerable interest to Parisian society; but, a good deal to my mortification, I discovered that I was the object of a good-natured but contemptuous merriment. I was a *balourd, a benêt, un âne,* and figured even in caricatures. I became a sort of public character, a dignity,

"Unto which I was not born,"

and from which I fled as soon as I conveniently could, without even paying my friend, the Marquis d'Harmonville, a visit at his hospitable chateau.

The Marquis escaped scot-free. His accomplice, the Count, was executed. The fair Eugenie, under extenuating circumstances—consisting, so far as I could discover of her good looks—got off for six years' imprisonment.

Colonel Gaillarde recovered some of his brother's money, out of the not very affluent estate of the Count and soi-disant Countess. This, and the execution of the Count, put him in high good humor. So far from insisting on a hostile meeting, he shook me very graciously by the hand, told me that he looked upon the wound on his head, inflicted by the knob of my stick, as having been received in an honorable though irregular duel, in which he had no disadvantage or unfairness to complain of.

I think I have only two additional details to mention. The bricks discovered in the room with the coffin, had been packed in it, in straw, to supply the weight of a dead body, and to prevent the suspicions and contradictions that might have been excited by the arrival of an empty coffin at the chateau.

Secondly, the Countess's magnificent brilliants were examined by a lapidary, and pronounced to be worth about five pounds to a tragedy queen who happened to be in want of a suite of paste.

The Countess had figured some years before as one of the cleverest actresses on the minor stage of Paris, where she had been picked up by the Count and used as his principal accomplice.

She it was who, admirably disguised, had rifled my papers in the carriage on my memorable night-journey to Paris. She also had figured as the interpreting magician of the palanquin at the ball at Versailles. So far as I was affected by that elaborate mystification it was intended to reanimate my interest, which, they feared, might flag in the beautiful Countess. It had its design and action upon other intended victims also; but of them there is, at present, no need to speak. The introduction of a real corpse—procured from a person who supplied the Parisian anatomists—involved no real danger, while it heightened the mystery and kept the prophet alive in the gossip of the town and in the thoughts of the noodles with whom he had conferred.

I divided the remainder of the summer and autumn between Switzerland and Italy.

As the well-worn phrase goes, I was a sadder if not a wiser man. A great deal of the horrible impression left upon my mind was due, of course, to the mere action of nerves and brain. But serious feelings of another and deeper kind remained. My afterlife was ultimately formed by the shock I had then received. Those impressions led me—but not till after many years—to happier though not less serious thoughts; and I have deep reason to be thankful to the all-merciful Ruler of events for an early and terrible lesson in the ways of sin.

ABOUT THE AUTHOR

Joseph Sheridan Le Fanu was born in Ireland in August of 1814. He studied law at Trinity College in Dublin prior to becoming a writer of mystery novels and gothic stories. His body of work is widely thought to have influenced other notable writers including James Joyce, Henry James, and Bram Stoker. Two of his most celebrated works are the mystery novels *The House by the Churchyard* and *Uncle Silas.*

www.ingramcontent.com/pod-product-compliance
Lightning Source LLC
LaVergne TN
LVHW090947080826
845145LV00003B/923

* 9 7 8 0 9 7 9 0 1 5 6 3 2 *